PLAY WITH MY HEART

A SOUTHLAND ROMANCE: BOOK 1

by
MEDA WHITE

Paperback ISBN: 978-1-941287-16-3

CHAPTER ONE

Liz Baker aimed her front kick at the middle of the wooden spindle and smiled when it detached, flying several feet to land on her brother's landscaped lawn. "This is so much fun. Thanks for inviting me to come for a visit and help replace your deck."

"Yeah, I can tell you like to kick stuff. You're not thinking of a certain man while you're doing that are you?" Danny stood off to the side, but splinters still flew too close to his head.

"No, I'm way past...him." Her ex-husband's handsome face flashed in her mind. She took out two slats at one time and pumped her fist in triumph.

Danny raised a brow. "Hmm. So you're ready to move on?"

"I didn't say that." Liz aimed another sidekick at a skinny piece of wood. "I may never be ready for that."

The pressure of a barrier slamming down in her mind to trap the hurt inside felt real. Compartmentalizing was a coping mechanism. Her ex-husband had broken her heart and crushed her biggest dream. As a result, she spent the three years following Jason's betrayal concentrating on her career. Her hard work paid off, but about the time she considered moving on, he came back into her life.

Liz wasn't dumb enough to take him back, but he wasn't looking for that. What he offered her was an explanation and a dream come true—albeit a different dream. They were amateur musicians who spent their youth writing terrible songs and plotting to put a band together. Once or twice a month, Liz got onstage at a little country bar near Atlanta to play her guitar and sing with her ex-husband and the band. She suffered no delusions that she was the next *American Idol*, but she loved to get lost in the music.

Music, its ability to move your soul, was something her biological father shared with her before his death. She'd been young, but it stuck with her through the years. Playing her guitar was a safe way to express the emotions she intellectualized the majority of the time.

Movement out of the corner of her eye from the house located behind her brother's home caught her attention. A man watched her from his own back door. She turned to tell Danny, but he'd just gone inside carrying the outdoor dining table over his head. Turning back toward the stranger, she noted he filled the frame of the doorway. Other than his size, she couldn't tell much about him...except that he might be blond.

She hoped he wouldn't call the cops. From his perspective, she might look like a woman hell bent on revenge by demolishing Danny's deck. She supposed her brother's Los Angeles neighbors didn't get to see many Southern women unleashed.

She stared right back at the man, waiting for him to make a move. In a moment, he checked his watch and turned away. She shrugged and went back to her task. They had to remove the old deck before they could replace it.

She meant to tell Danny about his nosy neighbor, but she forgot until a couple of hours later, when he strolled into the yard. "Hey, Danny, you've got company. Is it the HOA President coming to check your permit?"

Since Danny's house was in an affluent suburb, the neighborhood had strict guidelines about outside structures. The deck was about to fall down since it had been pressure washed to within an inch of its life, so he'd gotten his replacement plans approved by the powers that be.

Danny paused from prying up deck boards and adjusted his ball cap. "That's my neighbor, Ian."

"I'll run get us a couple of bottles of water." She laid her hammer down and headed for the door. He'd been spying on her earlier, it was time to repay the favor. Plus, she wanted to freshen up.

"Don't run. You might trip." Danny grinned at her and she tried to smack him on the arm, but he dodged her.

Once inside, she peeked out the window so she could see the newcomer without being seen. She wouldn't kick him out of bed for eating crackers. His clothes were suitable for the sunny May weather and showed off his well-built body in a snug-fitting, sleeveless blue T-shirt with khaki cargo shorts and athletic shoes. And she'd been right. He was blond and unfortunately, she had a thing for blonds. Her ex was blond. This guy was so attractive her insides sizzled like bacon in the iron skillet. But so was her ex and look where that got her.

Mr. Tall, Blond, and Built looked familiar; probably an actor she'd seen on television or in a movie. Whichever it was, good-looking was too mild a descriptor: The man had presence. L.A. was full of actors and actresses and her brother knew plenty of them, but Danny was the most discreet person in the free world. It was an important character trait for a guy in the security business.

The men talked while Liz dashed into the bathroom to check her makeup. She looked exactly like a woman who'd been doing outdoor manual labor. She straightened the brim of her Georgia Bulldog baseball cap, tucked a few loose strands of hair behind her ears and made sure her ponytail hung through the center in back. A little lip gloss and another dose of sunscreen on her fair skin and she was ready to face the gorgeous man outside. With her luck, he'd be gone and Danny would tease her for getting dolled up. But her middle sister, the quintessential Southern socialite, had always told her to put her best face forward. Old habits die hard.

CHAPTER TWO

Ian Clarke was disappointed that the long-legged lady who'd caught his eye this morning had disappeared inside as he approached. Admittedly, he'd been taken aback until he saw his neighbor present and laughing, amused by the woman's unconventional means of demolition. He'd relaxed and enjoyed the show until she caught him staring.

The jolt had reminded him of the appointment he'd needed to get to and the real reason he needed to speak to his neighbor, the security expert.

"Danny, mate. How are you?" Ian extended his hand.

"Good, just getting a little house work done. How are things?"

"Very well, thanks. Looks like a big project. Could you use some help?"

Danny's eyebrows disappeared under the brim of his cap. "Sure. Although I've recruited a professional, I could always use an extra hand." Danny passed him a lever bar, a tool that resembled a short, flat crowbar.

"Professional? Really? The legs—I meant, the woman?" Ian grimaced.

Danny smirked. "Semi-professional. And I'll thank you to keep the comments about my sister's legs to yourself. She's great at demo and construction, but when it comes to the heavy lifting, I'm on my own."

Ian was relieved to hear she was his sister because of his faux pas and because her legs had kept his mind occupied at his pre-operative appointment that morning. Lately, he'd surrounded himself with people to keep his mind off the upcoming surgery. When he was alone, he thought too much about keeping the nose bump he acquired during an ill-fated game of ice hockey. If it weren't for the deviated septum, he might not go through with it. He'd gotten his current television role with the imperfection which drew his eye every time he looked in a mirror.

"You talking trash about me again? I'm no weakling. See?" The sister curled the water bottles a couple times before she passed them each one with a big grin. "Hey, I'm Liz."

"Lizabelle, don't be jealous because this man can bench press me and not break a sweat."

She chuckled. "I'd like to see that."

"It's a pleasure to meet you, Liz." With the lever bar and water bottle in his dominant right hand, Ian shook her left hand and noted her long fingers and calloused fingertips. "I was about to tell Danny my show wrapped earlier in the week, and I have a little time on my hands."

"Thank the Lord. I was wondering who was going to help us with the two by twelves. You look...capable." Her eyes flicked from his arms to his face and her lips twitched into a smile as her eyes sparkled.

"Lizabelle." Danny's voice held a warning.

"What? It was a compliment. Clearly, he can deadlift more than me. But not much, I bet." Liz beamed at them both and went back to work, neatly stacking the deck boards Danny had removed and tossed haphazardly into a pile.

Ian grinned and stared as she moved into the garden. Her voice and accent reminded him of the way honey flowed from the jar, thick and slow. Her fair coloring was a big contrast to Danny's dark hair and olive complexion. He bet there was a blended family story there.

"Sorry about her, Ian."

"I don't see a problem." Ian followed Danny's lead and began prying up deck boards.

"We aren't blood kin, but I claim her most days." Danny smirked.

While working, Ian stole glances at Liz. The red-haired spitfire was like a breath of fresh, Southern air. She was removing nails from boards with a hammer and singing along to the radio. Seeing her up close, her big smile had momentarily stunned him. He wondered if it was the full lips or her easy manner that aroused his interest. The eyes didn't disappoint either, a turquoise blue he could swim in. She wasn't the typical gorgeous common to Los Angeles, but she had real beauty nonetheless.

"Danny, you told me a little about your business when we first met. Do you have any caregivers on staff by chance?" Ian was going for nonchalance.

Danny glanced up, then back down. "Nah, we specialize in bodyguards, security systems, weapons and combat training. It's funny you should ask though."

"Why?"

"My family's business, back in Georgia, is Home Health. Supplies, nurses, caregivers, you name it."

"Oh." Ian dipped his head and rounded his shoulders.

"You know someone with a need? It could possibly be an area of expansion for us at B & B."

Ian thought for a moment and let out a hard breath. He glanced to make sure Liz was occupied. "Can I speak frankly and be assured of strict confidence?"

"Absolutely." Danny looked at his sister and nodded to Ian.

"I'm having a medical procedure Monday morning and just found out I need a caregiver for a few days. Normally one night is all I'd need, but pain medications hit me hard. Because of my size, they always prescribe the highest dose. Weeks ago, my mum offered to come, but the surgeon made it sound so simple. In and out. So, I told her no. Now, it's too little time for her to change her plans and get here from London."

"Hmm." Danny rubbed his chin. "What's your need exactly?"

"Meals and medication. I've hired a car for the day."

"I'll take a break and make a few calls. No names. Just asking around." Danny laid his lever bar on the deck.

"I'd appreciate any assistance at all, Danny. They threatened to cancel if I don't have help and the timing is crucial, so I can be ready for the Season 3 premiere of my show next month."

Danny went inside and Ian continued to work. He

didn't have a plan B yet and he needed the procedure for his health—physical and mental—and to advance his career. He knew the big role that could launch him to a household name was just around the corner, and he'd be more likely to get it with a straight nose. If he had to lie or hire a beggar off the street, he'd do whatever it took. Nothing and no one was going to stand in his way.

After several moments of awkward glances, Liz stepped in and picked up where Danny left off. "You must've been really bored to want to help with this project."

"I suppose I needed a bit of stress relief." Ian said, tightening his grip on the bar to force a rusty nail free.

"You mentioned a show. What do you do exactly?"

Ian's head jerked up, eyebrows raised. "Have you not seen my show?"

She scrunched her nose and shrugged an apology. "I'm more of a reader. I hope you aren't offended." She was sincere.

"Of course not. I portray a doctor on *Trauma*."

"So, you're not a doctor, but you play one on TV?" Liz threw her head back to laugh at her own joke. "That must be why you look a little familiar. I've seen *Trauma,* but it's been a while. My neighbors invited me to watch a few episodes the first season. They still have watch parties."

"Did you not enjoy it?"

"Oh, Lawd." Danny had come outside.

"No, it's all right, Danny. I appreciate honest feedback. If you haven't noticed, most people in this town tell you what they think you want to hear." Ian was speaking to Danny, but his eyes never left Liz's face. His heart began to beat faster as she nibbled her lower lip.

Liz carried a deck board with both hands and tossed it onto the pile. "My reason for not being into your show says more about me than it does about you or the show."

"Let's have it then." Ian stood to face her.

"I'm not really into what my mama used to call smut." She held his gaze.

Ian pressed his lips together to hold the laughter in and looked to Danny, whose eyes closed and face turned red.

"Tell me you aren't undressed more than you're clothed." Liz put her fists on her hips.

"It's about fifty-fifty. I never thought of it as a problem, until now." Ian couldn't contain his smile and considered moving out of her leg's reach in case she was offended. But, he stood his ground.

"It's not a problem for most people," Danny said. "Liz is...modest."

"You say that like it's a disease, brother."

"If you ask me, there aren't enough modest people in the world," Ian said.

"That sounds like a load of bull, Ian." Liz narrowed her eyes.

He grinned like an idiot and tried to settle Danny down at the same time. "A woman who speaks her mind, you can't fault her for that."

He hadn't met an honest woman in a long time. Apart from his mum and sisters, the women in his life normally bent over backward to court his favor. Even his famous ex-girlfriend wasted a lot of false sincerity on him. Ian decided a Southern breeze might be exactly what he needed in his life, for the moment.

CHAPTER THREE

Liz stood almost toe-to-toe with the large man. Her dad and brothers were big men, over six feet tall, but this guy had them all beat. It was hard to look away from his blue-gray eyes. She loved the humor they held, even if he was laughing at her. She was sure most women would drop their drawers in a heartbeat if Ian fixed them with those eyes. *It's a good thing I'm not most women... although...* She nibbled her lower lip. Liz wasn't looking for love. In fact, she would run from it if it chased her, but a gal gets lonely and flirting with a Hollywood hottie never hurt anyone.

He smelled good too; even after working in the sun, there was a hint of manly soap. She refrained from leaning in closer to sniff him. Danny was already embarrassed by her blunt behavior. She tried to remember her manners. There was no need to run off the free help; especially, when he was so easy on the eyes.

She assumed most of the Hollywood types would have an aversion to manual labor, unless it was in the gym. Ian wasn't afraid of hard work and that scored him a few points in her book.

"You intrigue me," Ian said.

"Oh yeah?" Her eyebrows lifted and the bill of her cap did too, reminding her how tight it was.

"I saw you from my window this morning and wondered what kind of woman would kick down a deck?"

Her stomach did a dip and roll. Ian was intrigued by her and that made her nervous as all get out. "The crazy, Southern kind, I guess. Danny taught me self-defense, and I like to kick stuff when I get a chance, for practice, you know? He offered me a sledge hammer, but I thought using my feet would be more fun."

Liz passed the pry bar to Danny and went back to her hammer and her previous task of removing nails from the boards and stacking them in a neat pile. Ian was probably on the back side of thirty-five which would make him dateable since she was also in that vicinity age-wise. But, there was no way it would happen. He would never ask, especially since he could snap his fingers and women would come running—younger, skinnier, prettier women. Besides, being intrigued with someone wasn't the same as being interested.

Ian hinted he was stressed out and she wondered how stressful the life of a celebrity could be. In her mind, they all had personal assistants, chefs, trainers, and chauffeurs. She bit her tongue to keep from mocking the man and was surprised at how she judged him based on so little information.

Her mama's voice rang in her head, "Unless you've walked a mile in their shoes...." Liz chided herself and almost apologized to Ian out loud.

The trio worked companionably all afternoon disassembling the old deck. At one point, Ian grinned at something Danny said and although Liz didn't hear his comment, she was sure her brother had apologized for her again.

"Hey, Lizabelle, Ian has a big family, too." Danny unscrewed the top on a bottle of Gatorade.

"Yeah? How many siblings?" Liz wiped her face with the back of her arm.

"I'm the second of five children." Ian tossed a deck board onto the pile like it weighed nothing.

"I was the eldest of three until my mom married Danny's dad, then I became the second of six." Liz shook her fist in faux anger at her brother. "Is your family still in England?" She had a moment of panic when wondered if she misjudged his accent.

"If she bothers you with too many questions, just tell her to shut it." Danny slung a deck board in her general direction.

Liz dodged the plank and gave Danny the look they called the *stank-eye.*

"It's no bother. Yes, my family still resides in England. I miss them terribly, but for my career, it's important that I'm in Los Angeles."

"The Bakers are all still in Georgia, except for Danny. It can be overwhelming when we get together."

"Yeah, small doses makes them easier to swallow." Danny crossed his eyes and tossed another board onto the pile.

Liz loved her brother, but he often kept himself a little apart from the family. When their parents married, he resented having a new mom since he'd lost his to cancer and they'd been close. It was lucky Danny shared Liz's taste in music or they might not have connected. He'd been the one to convince his dad they needed guitars and lessons.

"Tell me about it," Ian said. "I have eight nieces and nephews and they think I'm a tree to be climbed."

I'd climb you. Liz put her hand over her mouth, worried she'd spoken out loud. Thankfully, she hadn't. "So, Ian, any other actors in your family?"

Danny shook his head. "Liz, what rock have you been under? Ian's dad is Simon Clarke."

Liz felt her face scrunch. "Sounds familiar." *Not really.*

"He's more well-known abroad than in the States," Ian offered with a glint in his eyes.

"You'd know his face if you saw it," Danny said.

Heat spread up Liz's neck. "I'm just gonna retreat over there and take my foot out of my mouth."

She was surprised Danny knew who Ian's father was, but he probably had all his neighbor's investigated before he bought in the neighborhood. Also, Danny needed to know who was who in the celebrity world since they were his clientele. Liz took a moment to be impressed by her brother the introvert.

When they decided to call it quits for the day, the sun was low in the sky. They'd removed all the old decking, leaving only the framework. Danny judged it to be a good foundation to rebuild on.

"Listen, a few friends are coming 'round tonight for a pint and a dip in the swimming bath. If you aren't too exhausted, stop over for a bit. You can unwind before bed. If not, I completely understand, and I'm happy to come again tomorrow, if you think you can use me."

Danny glanced at Liz for her reaction.

"Thank you for the invitation, Ian, but I'm still on Eastern Time so my bedtime was..." Liz paused to look at her bare wrist, "about ten minutes ago. I'm afraid I'll pass out very shortly after dinner." She turned to her brother. "Danny, feel free to go. I won't miss you once I'm asleep."

Danny stretched his arms over his head. "Depends on how I feel after she feeds me."

"You're gonna make me cook?" Liz put a hand on her hip.

Danny put an arm around her. "She's a great cook, so I always con her into making my favorite Southern foods when she visits. If I have any energy after dinner, I'll come drink a beer. Thanks again for your help today. Don't feel obligated, but we'd be grateful to have you back tomorrow."

"Think nothing of it. Happy to be of service. It was a pleasure chatting with you both." Ian strode back to his house.

"Hubba, hubba." Liz made a slurpy noise. "There's no way in the world I'm going swimming in front of him or his friends."

"What are you talking about?"

"I stretch the seams of my size eight jeans. Put me in a bathing suit next to size zero actresses in bikinis and call me *Moby Dick*."

"Stop that, you're *not* fat."

"Not in Georgia maybe, but we're in Hollywood. I'd be considered a plus size model out here."

Danny rolled his eyes. "Thanks for your help today and for giving me a pass to go over there. Maybe I'll meet a nice woman."

"As long as I'd approve of her, go right ahead." Liz paused and wrinkled her nose. "You're not mad at me, are you?"

Danny shook his head. "You've always spoken your mind, but you aren't mean about it. I love that about you."

Liz went inside to start dinner and realized that by not going, she wouldn't get to see Ian in a weenie bikini. She was a little disappointed until she remembered she could just watch *Trauma* and see pretty much all of him.

After they ate, she and Danny tuned their guitars so they could jam. Liz regretted declining the invitation because the thought of seeing Ian again excited her. She needed to get over it because there wasn't a snowball's chance in a Georgia July he would actually be interested in her. It could never be a thing anyway. He was a celebrity and she liked her mostly quiet life. She only let it get loud and crazy on her terms.

CHAPTER FOUR

While entertaining that evening, Ian was speaking with his co-star, Bryan Watson. "I helped my neighbor demolish his deck this afternoon."

"You're lying." Bryan was joking, but Ian walked him over to the edge of his lawn to show him the deck framework which remained.

"Dude, why would someone in this neighborhood do their own construction work?"

"He and his sister have done this type of work before."

"He has a sister?" Bryan raised his eyebrows. "Is she cute?"

"Yes, she is," Ian said. Then, hoping to divert Bryan from the topic of his neighbor's sister, he added, "Danny is former Special Forces or something and he does security and training."

"Man, you have to introduce me. My agent got me a script for a Commando part and I need to pick this guy's brain, you know, research the role." Bryan started walking into Danny's garden.

"Bryan, wait a moment. He may pop over later and if not, tonight might not be the best time to meet him.

I'm sure he's quite exhausted."

"I'll introduce myself quickly and tell him I want to hire him." Bryan went around the house to the front door since the back deck was impassable.

Ian followed Bryan and hoped he and his young co-star wouldn't be unwelcome.

"Hello again, Danny, I apologize for the intrusion, but Bryan insisted on meeting you straight away when I told him what line of work you're in." Ian shoved his hands in his pockets as he peered at Danny through the door.

"Come on in. Liz and I are just chillin'." Danny led them into the den.

"Are you listening to music? What band is this, man?" Bryan asked as they approached the room.

"That's Liz playing a Neil Young song," Danny said.

They entered the sitting room to find Liz seated on the sofa with her long legs stretched out on the ottoman in front of her and a guitar on her lap. She looked very relaxed and Ian assumed the beer bottle on the lamp table beside her had something to do with that.

"Wow, you sound great." Bryan looked her up and down. "That song is familiar."

Liz didn't get up, but she raised an eyebrow and kept playing. "Free beer if you can sing along."

Ian didn't sing but he spoke the opening line of *Down by the River*. "Be on my side. I'll be on your side, baby."

Her smiled broadened. "I knew I liked you."

"The first time I heard Liz play," Danny said, "she was trying to play along to *The Rain Song* on the most beat up old guitar I'd ever seen."

"What's *The Rain Song*?" Bryan asked.

"It's a hit by a little British band called Led Zeppelin," Ian answered before turning his attention to Liz and remembering her rough fingertips. "I didn't know you played. And Danny too, it seems." He gestured to the guitar lying on the sofa across from Liz.

"He's getting pretty good—almost as good as me." Liz set her guitar aside with a grin.

Ian squeezed his shoulder blades together to stop the flutter in his chest.

"That's a very sexy accent you have there, young lady." Bryan parroted her.

"You sure know how to flatter an old woman." Her accent was thicker than before.

"P-lease," Bryan said. "You can't be a day over thirty."

Danny stifled a laugh and Liz shot him a look which included a semi-serious raised eyebrow.

"It's getting deep in here y'all. Thanks, Bryan. I like you too. You might be my new best friend."

Bryan settled on the edge of the sofa and angled his body toward Liz. "You guys should come over to Ian's and have a drink with us."

Liz looked to Danny. "I guess we could go for a little while as long as Junior puts the shovel down." Her eyes cut to Bryan when she said the last bit.

"Hey, I'm twenty-seven and I don't have a shovel." He held up the beer in his hand and looked at Ian. "Do I?"

Ian's mouth twitched. "Apparently, Liz doesn't believe you to be sincere in your compliments."

She stood and Bryan mirrored her with a furrowed brow. "You can't be that old. What year were you born?"

Ian coughed, unable to believe his friend's imprudent question.

"I will tell you the song I was playing was before my time. Let's just say I'm old enough to know better, and too young to care. Didn't your mama teach you it's not polite to ask a woman's age?"

Ian was pleased Liz could stand up for herself and annoyed by his young co-stars flirtatious behavior. He'd seen him charm countless women and it had never bothered him before now.

Bryan launched into a conversation with Liz as they left Danny's house. He was trying to guess her age.

Ian slowed his pace to walk with Danny and spoke in a quiet voice. "We should keep an eye on him. Bryan has a reputation as a ladies' man. He enjoys the chase."

"He's no match for Lizabelle, she can handle herself. She'll eat him for lunch and pick her teeth with the carcass." Danny waved his hand to dismiss Ian's concern. "I have an idea about your situation."

"Oh?" Ian stopped to put more distance between them and Bryan and Liz.

"My days are booked this week and I don't have any employees who are qualified as caregivers." They continued walking.

"I knew it was a longshot—"

"Liz could do it," Danny interrupted. "She'll be here all week and she's a nurse."

"Really?" Ian rubbed the back of his neck and desperately tried to think of objections. "I..."

A rail-thin brunette with a name Ian couldn't recall approached as they entered his garden. "There you are, Ian. We wondered what happened to you." She put her hand on his arm.

Ian took her hand and put it in Danny's as he introduced them. Then, he maneuvered Bryan away from Liz. "Introduce Danny 'round for me, mate. Liz, would you care for a drink?"

"Sure, anything but the hard stuff." Liz followed him to the outdoor bar.

"I apologize for interrupting your visit with your brother and your jam session. I would love to hear you play."

"I'll have to talk Danny into it. He's shy."

"Is that how you earn your living then? Music?" Ian averted his gaze briefly.

Liz laughed. "Not hardly, music is my hobby. My day job entails boring computer stuff. I'm a closet geek, but don't tell anyone. It might ruin my cool musician vibe." She gave him a wink and he put his fist to his chest to stop the flutter again.

He couldn't fully understand how a simple gesture on her part could cause that response in him, except for it made him feel included in some private joke of hers. Women didn't normally share with him or he with them and that was for the best. He could take a woman to bed and not think about her much after she was gone, but he was getting the sense Liz wouldn't be so easy to forget.

"Indigestion?" Liz pointed to where his fist pressed against his sternum. "Apple cider vinegar is your friend."

It was the perfect lead in. "Are you also a nurse?"

Her grin widened. "Sometimes."

"I don't understand." Ian removed the cap from a beer bottle and gave it to her.

"I'm a visiting nurse when my parents need me. The experience helps me with my computer job."

"Are you a genius or something?"

Her face flushed as she cast her eyes down and turned away. "I'll take this to Danny."

"Allow me." He opened another bottle and followed her.

After making sure Danny was taken care of, Ian introduced Liz to another co-star and his wife who were also musicians. "I need to pop into the kitchen. Can I leave you here for a moment?"

Liz nodded. "Holler at me, if you need help."

Ian retrieved a fruit and cheese tray from his refrigerator while he thought about Danny's suggestion. He would have to be assured of confidentiality. He groaned inwardly because Liz was the first female he'd fancied since Emma. If she agreed to help him, she'd see him at his absolute worst.

When he stepped back outside, Liz was still talking with the couple he had left her with, standing on the far side of the pool. Bryan was rushing up behind her. Ian started toward them, but was too far away to warn her. He was amazed at what happened then.

Liz sidestepped and turned, tripping Bryan as she shoved him into the pool. Realizing what she'd done, her eyes widened and she sank to her knees by the side of the pool.

Ian joined her, fearing his co-star would react badly. Bryan intended to push Liz into the pool and having the situation reversed so abruptly might wound his pride.

Bryan came out of the water sputtering. "Wow, no one told me the sister was Special Forces too."

Tension eased from Ian's shoulders.

"I'm so sorry, Bryan. Are you okay?" Liz offered a hand.

Ian also offered a hand and together they pulled him out of the pool. "Are you quite all right, mate?"

"Fine. I was going to take a dip anyway. Did Danny teach you how to do that?" Bryan asked Liz as he took the towel she offered.

"That and more, my friend." She nodded.

"You're hired." Bryan shook Danny's hand.

"Sign me up," another person said.

"Do you have a business card?" someone else asked.

Danny had a cheeky grin on his face and spoke quietly to Ian as he reached for his wallet. "I told you she could handle herself."

Liz touched Ian's arm. "I'm gonna head home now. I've caused enough trouble for one night."

"You're no trouble at all." He placed a hand on her upper back and moved her away from the group. "I see it as a win-win. Bryan got knocked down a peg and Danny is getting a lot of business."

She winced. "I feel terrible."

"Please don't blame yourself." He resisted the urge to touch her again. "If you really want to go, I'll escort you."

"That's not necessary. I can take care of myself."

"I never doubted it, but it's late. I insist."

Liz told Danny and the others goodnight and gave Bryan a quick kiss on the cheek. Speaking of cheeks, hers were rosy pink and Ian knew they would be warm to the touch. He curled his fingers into his palms.

"I should've just let him push me in. Do you think he's really mad?" She scrunched her nose.

The urge to give her a comforting touch was strong, so he clasped his hands behind him. "He's a good sport if a bit rambunctious. I'm sorry he thought it would be a good joke to push you in."

"I don't think I could've done that if I didn't have three brothers and a pool growing up," she said as she walked beside him toward her brother's home. "You can imagine how many times I was thrown in."

Ian could envision it because his brother and he had done the same to his sisters.

When they reached the front door of Danny's house, Liz turned to Ian. "Thanks for the escort. Now, get back over there and enjoy your party. I hope I didn't ruin it."

"You couldn't ruin anything if you tried." Ian leaned in and kissed her cheek. It was warm.

"Next time, leave that shovel at home, ya here?" she said as a smile played at the corners of her full lips.

"One day, I'll pay you a compliment and you'll accept it."

"You're an actor. I might not believe anything that comes out of your mouth," she said with a smirk and raised eyebrows.

He tsked. "So cynical. I wonder what made you that way?"

Liz tilted her head to one side and her smile broadened as she shrugged. Ian was caught in it, forgetting what he'd even said. There was something about her. Not one thing, but many little things, all of which added up to something really unexpected.

"I've always been this way." She shrugged. "I think I should apologize. I didn't mean to criticize your career choice or how well you do it. I honestly don't know. But I Googled you and you've been at it a long time, so I bet you're pretty talented."

"You Googled me?" Warmth spread through his chest and his own smile broadened. It was ridiculous to be so enamored by this Southern belle. Women searched for him online quite frequently, but he didn't know those women. This one was standing a few feet away, breathing the same air. He was on the verge of asking her to dinner, but stopped himself just in time. If he couldn't think of another option, she might be his caregiver and she definitely wouldn't want to date him then.

CHAPTER FIVE

Liz and Danny were already at work when Ian arrived the next morning. Danny had asked for the details of her schedule for the week while he would be at work doing his day job. She planned to read, play her guitar, and get some binoculars to see if Ian sunbathed by his pool during the day. But she didn't admit the last part to her brother.

Her laptop was still in its case where she'd left it after looking Ian up online. Her cheeks warmed at the memory of admitting this to him. Because she worked as a software consultant, she could work remotely and arrange her schedule as she saw fit. She enjoyed the freedom and flexibility her years of hard work afforded her.

"Sorry I'm late," Ian said as he joined them. "My mum called for a chat."

"That's an excuse for a hangover I haven't heard before." Liz used a nail gun to attach additional supports to the existing deck framework as she calculated the time difference between the UK and California.

Ian smiled, but it didn't reach his eyes.

"Is everything okay?" Liz asked.

"All is well, nosy Parker."

"Hey, I'm armed over here." She posed *Charlie's Angels* style with the nail gun. "But you're right, I was being nosy, or concerned if you feel like being generous and putting a positive spin on it."

"The eternal optimist." Danny had already put brackets in the corners and was ready to bolt the outside frame. "You're just in time, Ian. Can you hold this board in place while I bolt it?"

The air compressor came on and Liz could no longer hear the men's conversation so she sang to herself. The boys worked concomitantly while Liz continued to measure, cut, and secure the brace boards in place. When the compressor went off, she could hear again, but pretended not to.

"Your sister is a pro with power tools." Ian held the two by twelve in place while Danny tightened the bolt with a socket wrench.

"Yeah, she has many talents. Makes me sick." Danny turned her way with a grin and stuck his finger down his throat.

Liz rolled her eyes at him.

"What is there besides carpentry, guitar, hand-to-hand combat, nursing, and computers?" Ian asked.

Danny glanced at Liz. "I'm surprised she told you about that." He changed drill bits. "The computer part."

Liz shook her head very slightly at her brother. She'd only mentioned it in passing to Ian and she didn't want any further details about her career shared with him or anyone. It wasn't like she was a hacker or anything illegal, but she'd rather people think that rather than treat her differently because of her success. She'd as soon avoid the subject altogether.

Ian looked over his shoulder at her. "She did say it was a secret of sorts. Didn't want to tarnish her reputation as a musician."

"Speaking of, Lizabelle, do you care if I invite Ian?"

"Not at all, the more the merrier." She lied and turned away because unlike Ian, she was not an actress and couldn't hide her insincerity.

Her stomach flipped — and not in a good way. She might have to back out. It was dumb to agree to play and sing in L.A. where there might be celebrities in the room. She scratched at itches which seemed to jump randomly from face to arm to leg and back again.

"We're going out tonight to hear a band at a place called The Rusty Roof. One of my buddies is the front man and Liz is gonna play a set with them. You ought to come with us."

"I wouldn't miss it. I have dinner plans, but I'll see to it we end up there." Ian bent to pick up a new deck board near. "Oh, and save me a dance."

Liz picked her chin up off the ground with an effort. Ian wanted to dance...with her. Her head itched like crazy. He was probably just being friendly, but truthfully she'd rather dance with him than play and sing in front of him. God never intended for her to be in the spotlight, at least not the bright ones in L.A. One reason for her uncommon case of nerves was because she was crushing on him. Realizing this made it worse. Her normal response under pressure was brazen and ballsy. When she felt an attraction to someone, she became shy and demure.

The same thing happened when she was around Chris, a guy back home she crushed on in school and beyond. Her friends told her to be herself and he'd ask her out. But fearing humiliation, she was afraid to speak in front of him. She dated him a few times after her divorce, but made a complete fool of herself. Ran him out of the state of Georgia.

She had a similar reaction the night of her Senior Prom when Jason stepped in at the last minute to be her date since her boyfriend had left her hanging. It was just Jason, Danny's best friend, whom she held brotherly affections for until he whispered in her ear he'd always liked her. In that moment, he was a stranger to her and she became a stranger to herself, unsure how to proceed. With time and effort, Jason put her at ease and eventually they proceeded down the aisle.

"Let's take a break, Lizabelle. Ian and I need to talk to you." Danny traded the nail gun in her hand for a bottle of water.

She looked to Ian who could barely meet her gaze. He crossed his canon-sized arms over his chest and then uncrossed them. She adjusted her shirt, followed Danny inside and sat at the eat-in bar in the kitchen. Danny leaned on the counter and Ian paced.

"What's up, fellas?" She took a big gulp of water.

"I want to hire you for a job," Danny said. "Discretion is of the utmost importance."

"Do I get to carry a gun?" Her eyes bugged out.

"Ah, no. That won't be necessary." Danny turned up one corner of his mouth. "You still have your California nursing license, right?"

"Yeah, why?" She'd worked as a nurse and gone to

school in San Diego when Jason was stationed there with the Navy.

"What I'm about to tell you must be held in the strictest confidence, whether or not you agree to the job."

Curiosity wasn't going to kill the cat, it was going to kill Liz if her brother didn't get on with it. He looked so serious. Ian did too.

"Agreed." She put the half-empty water bottle on the bar to indicate they had her full attention.

Danny nodded at Ian who spoke. "I'm having an outpatient procedure Monday morning. I've hired a driver for the occasion, but I need a caregiver for a few days."

"You can stay in one of Ian's guest rooms," Danny said. "You'll need to prepare meals, give him meds, possibly change bandages — you know, do that thing you do."

"I'd be happy to help, but I have a question." Liz clenched her icy fingers into fists as heat crept up her neck.

"Yes?" Ian asked.

"What procedure are you having?"

"Does it matter?" Danny asked.

"Yes. Anything below the belt and I'm out." Her work boots were suddenly interesting, her eyes searching them for any distraction at all.

"I'm having rhinoplasty." Ian wasn't smiling, but his eyes danced with laughter.

Danny tugged on his ear. "What would he have done…"

"Never mind, brother. I'll help you, Ian."

"Thank you. Since it looks like we'll finish the deck

today, perhaps you can come over tomorrow so we can discuss more of the details. I have prescriptions and pre and post-op instructions to follow."

"Absolutely, I'll do some research on my own to refresh my memory of the anatomy and physiology involved."

Liz was only slightly disappointed Ian's interest in her was as a caregiver. This scenario put them on more even footing, where she could forget the stupid crush and be herself. As they worked to complete the deck, her mind engaged in a new task of planning to provide the best care so Ian would suffer minimally and recover quickly.

She took a moment to watch him and wonder why he thought he needed his nose done. He was gorgeous just as he was. He caught her staring and offered her a tentative smile. She returned a smile and nodded before she aimed the next nail.

CHAPTER SIX

Ian scanned the crowded bar for Danny and Liz. Bryan was beside him, but their other friends abandoned them after dinner.

"I'm going to get a drink," Bryan said.

"Grab me a pint, won't you, mate, while I have a look 'round."

Danny sat at one of the small tables near the stage conversing over an empty chair with a pretty blonde when he spotted Ian and raised his bottle. Liz wasn't there, so Ian glanced around the dance floor as he made his way to his neighbor.

"I'm glad you made it." Danny introduced the woman as the girlfriend of one of the band members.

"Where's Liz?" Ian asked.

"Bathroom. Probably puking. She's going on in a few minutes."

A moment later, Liz touched Ian's shoulder as she passed behind his chair to sit in the empty seat next to Danny. A shiver ran through him.

"Nervous?" He asked as she sipped water.

"Very." Her hair hung straight past her shoulders and since Ian had only ever seen it up, it was lovelier than he imagined.

"Get out." Danny pushed her arm. "You do this all the time."

Bryan pulled up a chair and set beer bottles down for everyone before he moved to kiss Liz's cheek. "I hear you're gonna perform for us. When you're done, I need you to teach me how to do that dance." He gestured to the dance floor where couples were doing the Texas two-step.

Ian very nearly bowed up at his friend. The kid had nerve, but he also had no idea Ian fancied Liz.

"You want to wear the shine off my boots on the dance floor?" She asked with raised eyebrows.

Bryan grinned and nodded.

"Get in line, Junior. You can take me for a spin after Ian."

Ian suppressed his smile in time for the singer to invite Liz to the stage.

She stood and wiped her palms on her jeans. "Wish me luck."

"You don't need luck," Ian said.

"You've got this, Lizabelle." Danny fist bumped her.

"Pretend the audience is in their underwear," Bryan suggested.

Liz shook her head at them and took the stage. She wore a purple plaid Western-style shirt, tucked into jeans that hugged her curves and finished off the outfit with a pair of gray snakeskin cowboy boots. Ian noticed the silver belt buckle she wore as she put the guitar strap over her head. It featured a horseshoe; the same symbol he had tattooed on his right side where his elbow rested. The only people who knew he had it were his family, close friends and the makeup artists who covered it when he took his shirt off on set.

The drummer counted them in and Liz played lead guitar on *Sweet Home Alabama*. Ian leaned forward and propped his arms on the table. His gaze steady on her.

When he remembered to blink, he leaned toward Danny. "She's really good."

"The best." Danny agreed.

"Wow!" Bryan said. "Cute and talented."

"And too old for you, bro," Danny said. "Give it up."

"I'm just playing with her and she knows it. I haven't met anyone less interested in me." Bryan tipped his beer bottle upside down to drain it.

Ian almost felt sorry for his friend until he remembered who he was dealing with. Bryan only needed to look twice at a woman to get in her knickers. He had easy charm compared to Ian's cooler, British demeanor. Ian had been described as stand-offish, but having fame and money from a young age tends to make you wary of strangers. He found it easy to question people's motives and intentions.

The crowd applauded at the end of the song and Liz looked down to where they sat. Danny nodded his approval, Ian smiled his, and Bryan gave her two thumbs-up.

When the band launched into another song, Danny leaned toward Ian. "Not having second thoughts, are you?"

"About what?" Ian couldn't be sure if he meant the procedure or the caregiver.

Danny nodded at the stage and waited with a

cocked eyebrow.

"I don't doubt her ability. It's just..." Ian feared saying it aloud.

Danny took a sip of his beer. "It could be an opportunity for a man and a woman to get to know each other better."

Ian's smile creased his face. "I like the way you think, mate, but I fear she won't find me very attractive after the procedure."

"You're lucky she isn't overly concerned with what's on the surface." Danny settled back in his chair and returned his attention to his sister onstage.

A few songs later, Liz reclaimed her seat. "Is this for me?" She gestured to the beer bottle in front of her.

"Yeah, this Bud's for you, baby," Bryan shouted across the table.

"Don't call me baby, Junior." She snickered and clanked her bottle with his before she tipped it back. After several large swallows, she put the bottle down, covered her mouth and discreetly belched. "Excuse me."

Ian pressed his lips together to contain his smile. After a moment, he held out his hand to her. She took it and followed him onto the dance floor. He led her around the crowded floor absorbing details about the way she moved in his arms.

She looked heavenward. "Thank you, Lord, for sending me a man who knows how to dance."

"I took lessons at my parents' insistence."

"Be sure to thank them for me. My toes are grateful." The wink she executed was slow and intentional, aimed directly at his heart.

"Tell me about this." Ian touched her belt buckle,

running his thumb across the cool metal before he rested his hand on her waist.

"You know...horseshoes are good luck. When the ends are up, the luck is held in the curve. If the ends point down, the luck runs out."

"Do you feel particularly lucky this evening?"

"I'm the luckiest girl in this place." She beamed at him and he got lost in her smile.

When they got back to the table, Danny nudged him. "Way to sweep her off her feet."

Ian peeled the label off his beer bottle while Liz and Bryan joined the crowd on the dance floor. After a few mistakes, his friend got the hang of it.

"Thanks, Lizzie." Bryan dropped her off at the table. "I'm going to find someone to practice with."

"Uh-oh, *Lizzie,*" Danny said. "You've created a monster."

"I'm just glad he's looking for a playmate closer to his own age. And if you call me Lizzie again, I'm gonna spill my beer in your lap, accidentally on purpose."

"Hey, if Junior gets to call you Lizzie—"

"He doesn't know any better, but you do." She poked her brother in the arm with a finger.

Danny grabbed her finger and stifled a yawn. "I'm about ready to hit the road, Lizabelle. You've been working me too hard. I'm worn out."

"Might I beg for a lift?" Ian asked. "I rode with Bryan and it seems he won't be leaving anytime soon."

"Absolutely, let's hit it." Danny stood.

When they exited the bar, there was a line waiting to get in and cameras started flashing. Someone had called the paparazzi. Danny had bodyguard experience, so he tucked Liz behind him and pushed past the crowd to the parking lot. Ian followed closely behind with a hand on Liz's shoulder and stopped her from climbing into the back seat of Danny's truck. He maneuvered her into the front and got in the seat behind hers, thankful for the crew cab and the dark tint on the windows.

"You're not too cramped back there are you?" She asked.

"Not at all, there's quite a lot of space here. Nice truck, Danny."

"Thanks, man. It gets the job done. Liz just traded her old truck for one identical to mine."

Liz moved her seat forward. "Is that better? I know there's plenty of room back there for me, but I'm only five nine. You're what? Six-four?"

"Quite right. Why do you need a truck like this, Liz?" Ian leaned forward in his seat.

"Seven nieces and nephews. I don't usually have them all at once, but I can fit more of them in my new truck if I need to haul something."

"What do you *haul* in your truck?" The word was one he rarely said, but he really couldn't visualize her in a big truck, hauling things.

"I think he's making fun of me, Danny."

"I'm not, I swear. Just curious."

"Last thing I hauled was five hundred pounds of dog food to the hunting camp along with Nick, Jenny and Josh."

"Those are kids, not dogs," Danny clarified. "The bird dogs are at the camp."

Ian hadn't hunted since his youth and then he hadn't really enjoyed it. Being on horseback was the biggest thrill for him, but he did enjoy watching the dogs give chase.

Once they arrived at Danny's house, he thanked Danny for the ride and agreed to a time for Liz to come over.

"Goodnight and thanks for the dance," she said.

"It was my pleasure. We'll do it again when I'm well."

She nodded and turned to go inside. He enjoyed the sway of her hips. He had to change his thoughts if he was going to get through the next few days without making a pass at her.

CHAPTER SEVEN

Liz leaned against Ian's kitchen counter, reading the paperwork he'd received and making a list of supplies. She wanted to get cold compresses that wouldn't wet his cast since it needed to stay dry.

She lined up his prescription bottles after reading each label. She was familiar with the medications and their side effects.

He propped on the counter. "These knock me out."

"Me, too. I can't handle meds or drugs. Learned the hard way."

"Sounds like a story you can tell me while I'm recuperating." He smiled.

Liz stared at him a little too long and had to blink to break the spell.

"Okay, meals?" She turned away and opened the fridge. "You probably won't feel like eating and your mouth may be numb at first, but the pain medicine is best taken with food. If not, you may get nauseous and you aren't supposed to bend over, which is kinda necessary when you vomit."

"Are you trying to frighten me?" His eyes bugged.

"No, honey, I'm trying to prepare you. Don't worry,

we'll handle whatever happens. Do you have a protein shake you like?"

"In the cupboard." He opened the pantry door and showed her.

Liz read the list of ingredients to be sure it didn't contain anything which might react with his medication. She plundered for a few minutes to see what he had on hand so she could plan a menu.

"Can I see your bedroom?" She looked him in the eye and willed herself not to blush.

Her intentions were noble, but Ian flashed a wicked grin and headed down the hallway. She only checked out his butt part of the way.

The bed was king-sized and adjustable. He demonstrated then let her play with the controller.

"This is perfect. Since you can't lay flat, having the capability to raise the head of the bed will keep us from piling on ten pillows for the same affect."

Ian nodded, but she sensed he was still worried. She made it her mission to distract him as much as possible.

"Show me the bathroom. Where do you keep towels? Pajamas?"

Ian showed her around the house, including the guest bedroom where she would sleep. She hoped she wouldn't let him down...or Danny, who'd made her sign an employment contract for the job. He said he'd pay her, but she told him to donate it to charity instead. Besides, she didn't think Danny would actually charge Ian for the job.

Once back in the kitchen, Liz put Ian's papers in order and slid them into a drawer along with the prescription bottles as Ian went to answer a knock at the front door. He returned with Bryan in tow.

"Looks like I'm not the only one who got lucky last night." Bryan waggled his brows at Liz. "I owe you big time for teaching me those moves. I scored lots of numbers and a sexy little–"

"Bryan, that's quite enough detail, mate."

"Always happy to contribute to the delinquency of a minor," Liz told Bryan. "As if you needed any more mojo."

Bryan smiled and nodded and not for the first time, it struck Liz that while the kid had good looks and charm in spades, he either wasn't very bright or pretended he wasn't. She had personal experience with the latter, often downplaying her knowledge and abilities. Phrases like *scary smart* were common for a reason, and Liz had learned early in life that her I.Q. intimidated people.

"Hey, check this out." Bryan pulled his phone out of his pocket. "Your picture is on the Internet."

Acid burned the back of her throat as her stomach clenched. Ever since they left the bar the night before, she feared there would be an unattractive photo of her on the Web.

"Here's one of us dancing." Bryan held the phone so she could see.

Sure as shooting, there they were, nose to nose...or so it looked from the angle of the photo.

"You make me look short, especially when the next shot is of you and Ian." He slid his finger across the screen to reveal the picture.

Danny came in the back door and moved to look over her shoulder. It was a good picture of her and Ian in profile. He was looking down at her, she was looking up at him, and they both wore big smiles.

"Nice, Lizabelle." Danny nudged her. "Oh, and you too, Ian."

"You guys look good together." Bryan swiped his phone. "Here's one of you leaving the bar together."

Liz curved her shoulders forward and coughed. "Spitfire."

"Is that a problem?" Ian asked. "You don't have a beefy boyfriend back in Atlanta who'll be angry, do you?"

She shook her head and rubbed the back of her neck, unable to look at Ian.

"Check out the caption." Danny put his hand on her shoulder and squeezed.

It read: *Ian Clarke seen out with mystery woman. Let's hope he didn't trade Emma Stuart for this.*

"Rubbish," Ian said.

Liz laughed despite her compulsion to run from the room.

"I never read the captions." Bryan's lip curled. "They're either lies or just plain mean. Don't worry, Liz, I've met Emma and you're much sweeter than her."

Liz tried not to chuckle as her brother snickered. In his naivety, Bryan didn't realize saying she was sweeter than Emma, implied Emma was prettier. That was to be expected since Emma was a supermodel and Liz was a regular person. She just hoped the tabloids wouldn't do a side-by-side comparison of them because she was sure her sweetness would not be weighed in.

Ian tried to apologize for the photo and the caption.

"Ian, relax, it's not your fault." She touched his arm.

"I have no delusions that I'm a beauty queen. Plus, they don't know me. I'm just a random face. In a few weeks, they'll photograph you with another woman and I'll be forgotten."

"Not by me you won't." Ian looked her square in the eyes. "And you're wrong about not being a beauty queen. You're quite beautiful."

Her head dropped and heat infused her face as the full force of his direct compliment hit her.

Danny cleared his throat. "Ah, she meant the beauty queen thing literally. We have a sister who was a Miss Georgia finalist."

"Twice," Liz added.

"She's the beauty queen in our family, tiaras coming out of everywhere." Danny pretended to pull a tiara from his rear.

"Is she single?" Bryan asked.

Ian sighed, but Liz felt his eyes on her. She faked a smile and apologized to Bryan that both of her sisters were off the market.

"But our brother, Johnny, has a mean-ass ex-wife we'll give you. No charge," Danny said.

***

Ian let Liz in his back door early Monday morning. She smiled at the sight of him wearing the camouflage baseball cap she'd picked up for him the day before. It looked darn good on him, but then she was sure he'd look good with a paper sack on his head.

She'd been back in his kitchen the evening before unpacking grocery store purchases when she'd tossed him the hat.

He asked in a Southern accent, "You trying to turn me into a country boy?"

"It'd take more than camo to do that." She shot him a wink and a big smile.

He'd asked to go to the grocery store with her so he could pay for the food. She was gun shy about having been photographed with him, so his accompanying her was out of the question. She lied and told him Danny would pay and bill him.

"Is that what you're wearing?" She asked.

He looked down at his jeans and T-shirt. "Yes, why do you ask?"

"It might be tricky getting this shirt over your head when we get back. Do you have a button down you could wear instead?"

"Not one that goes with my cap, but I'll have another look. You're brilliant at this caregiver business."

Liz drove him in Danny's company SUV which had dark tinted windows. It was a Tahoe and since she also had the same vehicle at home, it was easy to maneuver through L.A. traffic.

He was nervous, if his foot tapping and finger thrumming on his leg were any indication.

She reached across the console and placed her hand on his. "It's not too late. We can turn back."

"No, it will be fine." His knee rocked side to side. "Won't it?"

"Your doctor is one of the best, so I'm positive you'll be happy in a week or two when the swelling goes down. Focus on the positive results."

"Right you are. I need this. No more sinus problems and it's only minor reconstruction. I'm confident I'll be pleased with the result. I guess I'm more concerned about the media—when they begin to compare before and after photos. I can't let it get to me. I should've learned to ignore them by now."

"Everything will be fine. The changes may be so subtle no one notices and if they do, who cares? As long as you're happy, that's what's important. And, you've got me to nurse you back to health, what more could you ask for?" She gave him her best cheesy grin.

He smiled and turned his hand over to squeeze hers. "Not to succumb from the anesthesia. But, I'm very glad you're with me. If I die, at least I'll die happy."

Liz kept her snarky comment to herself, but she briefly wished she hadn't left her waders in Georgia. Ian hadn't been bad about letting the bull crap get too deep, but he had his moments.

Liz passed the time while Ian was in surgery by re-reading the post-operative care instructions. She flipped through every magazine in the place, but she couldn't concentrate on their contents.

More than once, she'd wanted to ask Ian why, other than the septum repair, he thought he needed his nose reconstructed, but she tried to respect his privacy. She wished she could to tell him it wasn't necessary. His face would cause a nun to sin. But, it was his body, his career.

When the procedure was completed, a valet pulled the SUV around to the private entrance/exit reserved for celebrities and a male nurse helped her get him in the vehicle. She used a gentle tone and patted his shoulder. He was awake but drowsy, still feeling the effects of the sedation drugs although they'd made him walk on his own before they discharged him. The middle of his face was covered with a soft cast which would be removed at the follow up appointment in a week.

Liz wished Danny was around to help her unload Ian when they returned to his house. He was shaky on his feet so she put an arm around his waist and helped him to his bedroom.

"Dang, you're one heavy hunk of British beefcake." She helped him sit on the edge of the bed and kneeled to remove his shoes.

His hand patted her head, like a dog. "Liz."

He didn't have complete control of his speech because he held the 'z' for so long she almost swatted at a nonexistent bumblebee. Since he didn't have full motor coordination either, his heavy hand kind of hurt her neck.

"Yes, Ian, it's me." She took his hand and placed it beside him.

"I like you." He dropped his chin to his chest.

"Don't lean forward, honey. Sit up, head up." She adjusted the top of the bed to raise it and then leaned him back.

She gave him his medication and he made a mess, spilling the water down his shirt. After toweling him off, she started unbuttoning his wet shirt.

"You're undresshing me."

"Would you rather sleep in your clothes?" Her hand was poised over the next button.

He gave a small shake of his head indicating he didn't. Liz was tickled at the situation, but she didn't want Ian to think she was laughing at him so she pressed her lips tightly together.

She got the shirt down over his shoulders and helped him sit up so she could get it off. A horseshoe tattoo decorated the side of his torso. She wanted to ask him about it, but she'd wait until his mind wasn't drug addled. She tried really hard not to stare at his impressive physique. When she leaned him back again, she sighed. People shouldn't look good enough to cause nuns and nurses to have impure thoughts. His body was a work of art, but she'd have to admire it later...after she got the jeans off. She should've suggested sweat pants.

"Ian, sweetie, I need you to stand so I can get your pants off. You can lean on me if you feel dizzy."

"I'm too heavy...beefcake." The sound he made was probably supposed to be a laugh, but it sounded like the hogs after slop.

"Um..." She pressed her lips together. "Okay, I'll try to do it with you lying back." She lowered the bed a little.

When she unbuttoned his pants, his eyes popped open and he put his arms around her, pulling her down on top of him. Laughter bubbled up and she shook against him trying to contain it.

"Ian." She tried to wriggle out of his grasp, but his arms were apparently lead-filled. She started sliding down his body hoping to find an escape. The friction caused a physical reaction in him which was unexpected, given that he was completely lax.

No more Miss Sweet Thang, she was going to have to get tough. "Ian, let me up."

He lifted his head and looked at her. "Are you going to take advantage of me?" He asked in a clearer voice than he'd used since they'd gotten home. "I won't object."

She pushed his arm and his grip loosened so she

could roll off the man and the bed to freedom.

"We'll just leave the pants on." She averted her gaze as she adjusted the pillows and then covered him with a blanket.

The wingback chair next to the bed was calling her name, so she plopped down for a much-needed rest. His liking her and the full frontal body rub was unforeseen. She took a moment to appreciate her predicament as Ian's snores began to fill the silence.

CHAPTER EIGHT

Ian awoke to a sound by his bed. He tried to open his eyes but the pain was beyond belief. "Bloody hell, what have I done? I'm blind."

"You're not blind, sweetie. Your eyes are swollen and they may get worse before they get better, but I've been applying cold compresses to help."

"In future, when I tell you I'm having plastic surgery, just shoot me instead."

"It's a good thing Danny wouldn't let me carry a gun." She squeezed his shoulder. "Time for meds. Do you want a cold shake or warm broth and crackers?"

The roof of his mouth was a little numb and the thought of something cold made his face ache from the inside out. "Broth."

Liz raised the bed higher and adjusted his pillows. Her gentle touch on his bare torso gave him a momentary distraction from his discomfort. She helped him sip warm broth and she fed him crackers, brushing crumbs from his lip with her thumb. He hadn't realized the situation would be so intimate.

After he'd taken the medication, he needed help to the loo, but was reluctant to ask.

"Do you need a pit stop?"

"Are you a mind reader?"

"No, but you're pinching your knees together like my nephews do when they have to pee real bad. I'll help you to the toilet but then...." Her voice trailed off.

"I can take it from there."

She helped him stand and put her arm around his waist. *I rather like this*, he thought, but didn't dare say it out loud. He didn't want to make her uncomfortable.

Once she deposited him in the small water closet and closed the door, he leaned against the wall and considered aiming from there. He could barely see and he didn't want Liz to clean up errant urine, so he sat down to relieve himself.

From his seated position, he removed his jeans, but held onto his boxers. No need to flash Liz if he couldn't enjoy her reaction. He stood, flushed and opened the door.

She took his jeans from him, then helped him wash his hands. "That's enough. Avoid the mirror."

He patted his hands on a towel she held. "I look like a reject from Frankenstein."

"It's only temporary. You'll be back to your handsome self in no time. Do you want to change into pajamas?"

He smiled on the inside. "It's beyond my ability at the moment."

"No worries, boxers make good sleep shorts." She held onto his arms as he sank onto the bed. "Your mom called, by the way. I hope you don't mind that I answered your phone. It said *Mum* on the display. She was worried about you."

"I don't mind. Thank you, Liz. I couldn't survive

without you." His muscles relaxed completely as soon as he settled onto the pillows with her assistance.

It wasn't long until he drifted off again. He dreamt of music and a beautiful ginger. He awoke frequently and each time, he groaned when he remembered what he'd done. Sometimes, he spotted Liz seated in the chair near his bed before he drifted back to sleep. Sometimes, he'd feel her touch and hear her gentle voice.

The next morning, he was awake when she set the breakfast tray on the nightstand.

He squinted at her. "Did you play your guitar while I slept?"

"I hope it didn't disturb you." She sat next to him. "I refrained from playing heavy metal."

He wanted to smile, but his face hurt. "Soothing." He raised the bed. "I need the loo before food."

Remembering he wore only boxers, he cautiously pulled back the covers. Liz turned away to get his robe and then helped him get his arms into the sleeves. He pulled it closed before he stood.

"Will you get my pajamas, please? I can dress while seated on the throne, so to speak."

"I didn't know you were a Royal." Liz laughed at her own joke and he grinned in spite of the pain.

While he sipped his protein shake, his mum called again.

"Mum, I hear you've been checking up on me."

"Yes, dear, how do you feel?"

"Terrible."

"Put Liz on."

He hit the button for speaker and lay the phone in his lap. "She's here."

"Elizabeth, darling, how does he look?"

"Like he lost a boxing match." Liz patted his leg.

"Can you send me a picture?"

"No, ma'am. Too many things can go wrong when sending photos over the digital air waves. I'm sure Ian will send you a picture after his two-week appointment when the color is normal and edema is gone."

"I understand completely. I'm pleased you're there to care for my son."

Ian was impressed. Liz handled his mum and his situation with aplomb and discretion. He released a satisfied sigh and for the first time, the peace in his heart diminished the pain in his face.

After a few more questions, answers and reassurances between them, he disconnected the call. "I think she likes you."

"Only because I'm taking care of her number one son. She's very sweet."

"She is that, sweet and beautiful– like you."

Liz slid down in the chair. "Yesterday, she wanted me to serve you tea and biscuits, but I told her no caffeine this week. I get the feeling that what she calls a biscuit and what I call a biscuit is not the same thing."

Tightness in his cheeks stopped his smile short. "Biscuits are cookies. They're in the cupboard. Help yourself to them, if you like."

"I don't need cookies or biscuits." Liz removed the breakfast tray and left him to rest.

***

Ian awakened alone and checked the time just before Liz entered the room with another tray of food.

"All I do is eat and sleep."

"Your body is healing while you rest. Enjoy the down time. I'm sure you don't get it very often."

"Why are you so good to me?" He asked.

"Because, you might fire me if I'm not."

"Never. I can see a bit better now, perhaps I can try feeding myself this time."

Her eyes sparkled when she smiled and he didn't want to look away. "Sit with me, just in case."

She sat in the chair by the bed and looked at home there.

"Comfy?" He asked.

"Yes, this chair has molded itself to my behind. We're old friends by now."

"I thought I was dreaming of you there." He gestured to the guitar on the stand beside it. "Will you play for me? Now that I'm conscious and can actually enjoy it."

She played a soft song with a melody he recognized, but couldn't name. He held his eyes open to watch her fingers thrum the strings until the weight of his eyelids forced them closed. The music stopped and a moment later, the cold compress settled on his eyes. The corners of his mouth turned up and he fantasized about her becoming a more permanent part of his landscape.

***

After dinner, he needed conversation. "Tell me more about yourself, Liz."

"Um...there's not much to tell really. You already know about my mad guitar skills and that I'm a computer nerd."

"What about your family?" He hoped to eventually get around to his real question.

"We're the Baker's half-dozen. My mom married Danny's dad, six kids, the Brady Bunch minus the bell bottoms."

"Did you have an Alice?"

"We have Aunt May and Uncle Ben Hill. She's the housekeeper and he's the groundskeeper."

"It's a large estate?"

"Yeah. Southland sits on several hundred acres. There're three guest cottages, a pool, lake, shooting range, a dozen horses, corral, stables, you know, all the stuff Southerners love."

"Your father is wealthy then?"

Her spine stiffened and her face closed down. Her friendly smile and easy nature became guarded. "He does alright. You have to realize that the cost of living in rural Georgia is much lower than here in California."

"I see. I offended you. I'm sorry."

She shrugged and leaned back in the chair. "You didn't. I didn't mean to brag about where I grew up."

"You mustn't apologize for being proud of where you came from, Liz. I didn't consider the cost of living you mentioned."

Ian thought a change of subject was in order, so he went directly to the thing he wanted to know most.

"Why are you not married?"

Her eyebrows rose and a smile played at the corners of her full lips. "Who's the nosy Parker now?"

"I admit it. I'm interested to know how someone as kind and beautiful as you are, isn't taken."

While she considered her answer, she leaned her head against the side of the chair. He was an idiot to ask about her love life when his face could cause children to have nightmares, but he didn't know how many days he had with her and he wanted to make the most of his time. She'd agreed to play it by ear, according to how he felt and he thought he might not feel very well, very soon.

"I'm divorced. I was married for a little over a decade, but it didn't work out."

"Your ex-husband cocked it up then?"

She laughed. "You could say that."

"What happened...if you don't mind telling me?" He hoped he wouldn't push her away by asking.

"We got married right out of college. He was a pilot, first in the Navy and later commercial. He told me about the other woman when she thought she was pregnant. When given the choice, he picked her."

"You tell the story so unemotionally. You must have been heartbroken?"

"It was five years ago and I was devastated. I never imagined he would betray me that way. Not only me, but Danny and the rest of my family."

"What do they have to do with it?"

"Jason, my ex, was Danny's best friend. Still is... sorta. They grew up together and he was just like another brother until he stepped in to save the day at my Senior Prom."

"Tell me about prom."

"I don't know how they do it in England, but in Georgia it's a big deal. Girls spend months shopping for dresses and shoes. Oh, and get this, my boyfriend didn't want me to be taller than him so I had to wear flats. Cute heels are the best part. Anyway, he dumped me the week before prom and I threw the flats in the trash. I dug them out later because Aunt Nancy liked them and Big Daddy threatened to take me to the woodshed."

Ian tried not to laugh. He had so many questions. "Wait, how tall was this boyfriend?"

"Maybe, two inches taller than me." She shrugged.

"Why'd he dump you?"

"He was a freshman in college and thought he was too mature to go to a high school prom. It was a good thing he told me over the phone, 'cause I might've clawed his eyeballs out if he'd been in front of me."

"Remind me to never make you angry. You have a dangerous front kick and claws I wasn't aware of."

She nodded with narrowed eyes. "You got that right, mister." The serious look faded into a big smile. "Anyway, Jason, who was a freshman at Georgia, was at Southland when I got the call. He offered to take me to prom, so I got high heeled shoes and swore I'd never date another man under six feet tall."

"So, prom night was the beginning of something with Jason?"

The faraway look in her eye let him know she was in another place and time. She nodded. Ian almost asked if she still loved him, but he didn't really want to know the answer. Those sorts of feelings were complicated.

"Why would Danny remain friends with him after he betrayed you?"

She let out a long breath. "He didn't. They only recently reconnected and that was my doing. It turns out there were extenuating circumstances and when Jason explained them to me, I talked Danny into giving him another chance. The rest of my family has been slower to let him back into the fold."

"I don't understand."

"I can't say more. Everyone thinks I'm an idiot for forgiving Jason, but I don't care. Forgiveness let me out of a self-imposed prison."

Ian pondered her words a moment. "You have no wish to reconcile with him?"

She twisted her mouth. "I can forgive, but forgetting isn't so easy. I don't think I'd ever be able to trust him again."

"And why have you not remarried?"

"Why aren't you married, Ian?"

"Haven't found the right woman and I'm putting it off until my career is better established. My sights are set on the big screen. With luck, I'll get to the place where I can choose my projects."

"So you're putting your personal life on hold while you chase your dreams?"

"I suppose. There's also the fact that I don't want children so I don't see the need to rush to the altar."

Her face paled, but she turned away, leaving him to doubt what he'd seen.

"I'm sure it sounds ridiculous, but growing up in the spotlight as the child of a celebrity and then working from a young age is not the fun it's cracked up to be."

"I think you turned out all right."

"My siblings all have normal lives, but I...I'm terribly insecure about my acting ability. I feel as though I always have to prove myself."

"Everyone feels that way. I had to prove myself in my field; Danny did in his."

"But in my field, my success is credited to nepotism and the world is watching to see if I fail."

"Yeah, I don't think I could handle that. I prefer to

fail privately, but if you feel that way, why act? Why not do something innocuous, like banking?"

"I started acting as a child and once the bug takes hold of you, it's hard to think of anything else. I took a break to go to university, but I never imagined I'd do another job. It's always been my dream."

"It sounds like you do it because you love it. If that's the case, then you have all the confidence you'll ever need. Take that passion with you to work and it'll come across on screen."

"Thank you for the words of encouragement, but I'm curious about something. You clearly love music. Why not pursue it? And how did you turn the conversation around like that?"

She smiled a smug, tight lipped smile. "It's a gift and my music is for fun, for me. It keeps me connected to someone I lost."

"Your father?"

She nodded.

Ian stopped pressing as exhaustion tugged at him, but he wanted to know more. He wanted to know everything; every hope, every fear. Being near Liz satiated something deep inside him.

CHAPTER NINE

The next morning, Liz anxiously delivered Ian's breakfast. She'd barely gotten out of revealing some of her most closely guarded secrets the night before during the British inquisition. She hoped his curiosity was satisfied.

"I have a goal for today." He adjusted the bed. "I desperately need a bath."

"I didn't want to say anything, but…" She grinned. "I'll run the water while you eat." She paused on the way into the bathroom. "You can wash yourself, right? You didn't mean that you want me to bathe you?"

"You can if you like. I may need help with my hair."

"Um...maybe you should skip the hair for today. I have dry shampoo. I'll hook you up after your bath."

"But if I'm already in the bath, won't it be easier to just do it then?"

On her nursing rounds, she'd bathed countless men and helped them pee, but they'd all been elderly. Her heart beat harder imagining him in the tub. "Um, I think it'll be hard to keep your face dry while washing your hair. We can't risk wetting the cast. Maybe we can lay you back over the kitchen sink later, when you have pants on."

"Now that I know you were married, I'm rather surprised male nudity is such a problem for you."

Her face got hot and she turned and made her way toward the bathroom to run the water. She couldn't help it. She wasn't comfortable with her own nudity...or anyone else's.

Just because the rest of the female population enjoyed seeing Ian in the altogether didn't mean she had to join their ranks. *What is wrong with me*? She should want to see his glorious body and part of her kind of did, but warning bells rang. Caution! Seeing Ian unattired will lead to sexual frustration.

Once she had the bath ready, she returned to get him.

"I'm sorry I made you uncomfortable. The dry shampoo will be fine. Perhaps tomorrow, we can attempt the kitchen sink idea."

"Deal." She kept her eyes down.

He was steadier on his feet today, so she didn't have to help him as much. She got him a clean pair of pajama pants and put them in the bathroom along with a towel.

"I'll be out here if you need me."

She changed the bedding and remembered Ian's words about her taking advantage of him. She was sure he didn't remember anything he said that first afternoon. If she were *that* kind of girl, this would be the perfect opportunity. But she wasn't, so she wouldn't have any stories to tell the grandchildren she'd never have.

When Ian emerged from the bathroom wearing

pajama pants and nothing else, Liz struggled to keep her attention on her guitar. She licked her lips and swallowed a few times, unsure what caused the excess saliva. She didn't have to look at her hands while she played, but that's what she did since her body reacted inappropriately to his proximity. It was wrong for nurses to want their patients. Wasn't it?

"I'm going to watch the telly for a bit." He adjusted the head of the bed.

She held the pillows in place while he settled against them before she left for the kitchen. When she returned to check on him, he turned the TV off.

"My eyes still hurt, but I'm a bit bored. I'm tired of sleeping." He tugged at the gray striped comforter.

"Do you like audiobooks? It's kind of like watching a movie, but you can do it with your eyes closed."

"Brilliant."

She got her phone and shared her audiobook collection. "I can also download something else."

"Let's hear the one with the vampires, they're all the rage."

"It's all fun and games until they sink their fangs into you." She attached the auxiliary cord to his docking station and started the book.

Several chapters in, Liz sensed a descriptive love scene about to unfold. She couldn't run from the room in embarrassment, so she bit her lip and tried not to blush. Before it was over, she covered her face with her hands. The narrator stopped and she peeked between her fingers to discover Ian had paused the book.

"I need a cigarette." She fanned her face with her hand.

"You really are quite modest. It's refreshing to see a woman blush. It's my belief that the women I work with don't think twice about such things."

Liz usually got teased about her modesty, but Ian appeared sincere in his compliment. Maybe Danny was right, she just needed to get desensitized.

"Do you need a break?" She asked.

"That's how you do it. You redirect the conversation. Very subtle."

"I'm not sure you're complimenting me now, so I'll go get lunch ready." Liz was surprised when Ian followed her to the kitchen.

"If I stay in bed, I'll go back to sleep." He slid onto a stool at the counter. "May I help?"

"You can help by taking it easy," she said, just before his phone rang. "Tell your mom hello for me."

After lunch, Liz could tell he was getting tired because his shoulders slumped and he rubbed the back of his neck repeatedly.

"Back to bed. You need to rest." She pulled his hand to help him to his feet.

He fell asleep right away and she sat in the chair next to his bed admiring him. Even with a cast covering part of his face, he was very handsome. It was the eyes and the body, not to mention he was a sweetheart. His chest rose and fell with his breath and she imagined laying her head there. Her head had been there for a hot minute, but she'd been trying to escape at the time. If it happened again, she'd savor the experience.

His snoring problem was improving which meant the swelling was decreasing. She looked forward to seeing him when the cast came off, if he'd let her. She might not have an excuse to be in his life then.

***

Ian woke in time for dinner and afterward they listened to more of the book. He admitted it was entertaining. The narrator did a fantastic job with the characters' voices.

He was a bit concerned he had frightened Liz with his questions the day before. He wanted to know her better but to what end, he wasn't yet certain. She clearly wasn't the type of woman to have an affair. In truth, he was glad of it. He liked her more because he knew she wouldn't shag him or any other man unless she had real feelings for them.

He noticed Liz stifle a yawn and realized they'd been listening to the book for several hours. He stopped it for the evening.

"You look like you could use some rest. Have you not been sleeping well?" He asked.

"Not really. I've been worried you might need something at night and might try to take care of it on your own."

"You've been sleeping in my chair, haven't you?" He shook his head as her ears reddened.

"Maybe a little." She shrugged.

"I should scold you, but I appreciate you too much. If you find you have trouble sleeping tonight, there's plenty of room in my bed. It's a king you know, gives me plenty of leg room."

Her yawn transitioned to a grin. "Thanks, but you seem much better today and I'm so tired, I might just sleep through tonight. But, please, call me if you need me."

"All right, but the offer stands if you change your

mind. You're safe with me."

She mumbled something unintelligible.

"What was that?"

"Nothing. Sweet dreams." She waved with one hand and covered a yawn with the other as she shuffled out of his room.

"Tomorrow, we attempt to wash my hair." He called after her.

He lay there thinking about Liz for a long time. He hadn't dated anyone seriously since he broke it off with Emma before the New Year. She'd been furious and called him every name in the book on top of telling him he couldn't act to save his life. Her unkind words reignited his feelings of inadequacy as an actor and he'd been struggling to put them out of his mind ever since.

Liz had been kind and encouraging, but she hadn't seen his show. He wondered if she was wishful thinking or if she really had faith in his talent. A man needed the support of a good woman. Liz might be the woman, but it was too early to know for certain. She probably wanted kids and since she was in her late thirties, she'd need to get cracking if she intended to have even one. That wouldn't work into his plan, so he pushed her out of his mind.

When he finally drifted off to sleep, he dreamt of a red-haired woman holding a little blond boy.

CHAPTER TEN

Liz opened her eyes the next morning to find Ian looking at her from his place on the bed. She sucked in air and proceeded to fall backwards off his bed. The landing knocked the breath out of her.

"Liz, are you all right?" Ian rounded the end of the bed.

"Don't bend over." She struggled to breathe. "I'm fine."

"I see you took me up on my offer to share the bed." He towered over her and rested his hands on his hips.

"I meant to wake up and be gone before you knew I was here."

"Don't be embarrassed. You only snore a little."

She closed her eyes, wanting to disappear. "Lord, have mercy."

Ian Clarke heard her snore. It occurred to her she could crawl under the bed and hide, but that would make things worse. Well, she'd heard him snore too and very loudly in the beginning, but she didn't intend to tell him. Just like she didn't intend to tell him the things he said when he was drugged. He wasn't in his right mind then.

"Here, take my hand." He held it out for her.

She opened her eyes and pushed herself up as he pulled. She was on her feet in an instant and because he was so strong, he pulled harder than necessary. Her face crashed into his bare chest and his arms went around her to steady her. When she'd imagined her cheek resting there, it had been much gentler and more sensuous with less probability for whiplash.

She remained frozen in place, in his arms, willing her feet to move, but they wouldn't obey. The heat of his body seeped through her tee shirt and she resisted the urge to sigh.

He moved his hands from her back until they held her upper arms before he moved back a half step so he could see her. "Did you hit your head?"

I wish. Then I'd have an excuse for my ridiculous behavior. "I don't think so." She felt the back of her head. "No, I'm good."

His eyes narrowed. "Come, sit for a moment."

He kept a grip on one of her arms as he led her to the chair she wished she'd slept in like all the nights before. If it was possible to die of mortification, she'd be a goner. He sat across from her on the bed and scrutinized her.

"I'm fine, Ian, really. I'm embarrassed you busted me sleeping in your bed. I wasn't trying to take advantage of you, I promise. And to top it off, I fell out of bed, which is even more embarrassing."

He took her hand. "I invited you to sleep in my bed. You weren't breaking any rules. I know you'd never take advantage of me. That's just silly."

She pressed her lips together at that statement.

He continued, "I'm sorry you fell out of bed and I hope you're not hurt."

Standing quickly with her eye on the door, she said, "Only my pride. I'm going to get dressed and see about breakfast."

***

After taking the world's fastest shower Liz got dressed and headed straight to the kitchen, avoiding Ian's bedroom in the hopes of avoiding him. When she reached her destination she found to her dismay that he was already there, making coffee for her. He'd traded his pajama pants for shorts, but he was still shirtless. *Look away from the sculpted body.*

After they ate, Ian was ready to get his hair washed.

"I thought we could put a stool in front of the sink. You can sit and lean back against the edge of the counter. I'll put a towel there to make it more comfortable." Liz patted the counter.

He stood. "Let's crack on, shall we?"

She gathered the supplies. This would require close contact, so she was glad she showered. There's nothing like having your armpit in the face of a hot actor, even if his nose might not be fully functional.

Once he was leaning back, she held up a washcloth. "I'm going to cover your face with this in case you get splashed. This is my first time as a shampoo girl, so the results are not guaranteed."

"I trust you."

She placed the cloth over his eyes and wished she had more time to gawk at his body. Hot diggity. His abs were fully engaged and she imagined tracing the ridges with her fingertips. She wiped some drool from the corner of her mouth before she proceeded.

She warmed the water to a comfortable temperature and used the sprayer to wet his hair. With one hand, she sprayed and with the other, she cupped and deflected the water. She released the nozzle and grabbed the shampoo.

She basically did what the salons did. She always loved getting her hair washed at a salon; it was like a scalp massage and it never felt quite as good when you did it to yourself.

She rinsed and repeated with the conditioner. After the final rinse, she reached for the towel Ian held in his lap, but he tightened his grip on it.

"I'm sorry, but I can't let you have this towel."

"Why not?"

"Trust me on this, you don't want this towel. Use the one under my back." He lifted himself off the counter.

She quickly grabbed the towel and used it to soak up the moisture.

"I can take it from here." He stood taking the damp towel from her with one hand while he kept the dry one firmly in place over his lap.

Well, lookie there, Nurse Baker. She fought a smug smile even as she blushed.

"I'm sorry," she said to his back as he went to his room and closed the door.

She hadn't meant to do it, but she felt a little bit happy she had that effect on him, twice. Of course the first time, he was whacked out on a sedation cocktail and the second...well, for all she knew, it happened every time he had his hair washed.

The water was running in Ian's giant bathtub so she knew he'd be occupied for a while. She texted Danny and invited him over for dinner. If Ian wanted her to, she'd go back to her brother's house, but she secretly hoped he needed her to stay.

***

Ian sank down into the warm bath. Liz had only some idea of how she had affected him. The feel of her hands on his head and the scalp massage was bloody fantastic. He was getting aroused all over again at the memory. Her scent, an earthy citrus combination, lingered in his mind and threatened to overwhelm him. If he had not been mending from surgery, he would have made a serious attempt to gain her affection.

He still might make the attempt, but the physical relationship would have to be put off until he was well. Who was he kidding? She wouldn't jump into a physical relationship anyway. He'd have to let her lead. If and when she was ready, she'd have to let him know. For now, he'd continue getting to know her.

Wanting to give Liz some space, he sat in bed watching the telly for a bit. His mum called and she sounded glad to hear he was much improved. He assured her Liz was taking great care of him and keeping him entertained.

"She sounds delightful, Ian. I'm so pleased you have her."

Ian thought his mum misunderstood the situation, but before he could set her straight, she had to go.

Just as he ended the call, there was a knock at his bedroom door. He called for Liz to come in as he moved to answer it.

Liz opened the door while trying to balance the serving tray on her knee. It was a disaster waiting to happen and Ian couldn't get there fast enough to help her and prevent the tray from tumbling out of her grip and onto the floor. They both bent to try to set things right. Liz backed away and sat on the floor in the hallway.

"Is something the matter?"

"Don't bend down, Ian." Her voice was harsh until she softened it with, "Please."

He stood back up. He was feeling much better because he hadn't thought twice about bending over to help her and he should have.

"This is why I'd never make it as a waitress." She smiled. "I'm sorry, but I didn't want to head-butt you in the face."

"Thanks for that. I'd forgotten I left the door closed. I wasn't trying to shut you out."

"I'm sure you miss your privacy. I'll go back to Danny's when you say the word."

"I don't want you to go."

She righted everything on the tray and picked it up to take back to the kitchen. He followed and got dishcloths and a roll of paper towels to clean the floor.

"Give me." She took the supplies from his hands. "I'll be right back."

He stayed behind in the kitchen and decided the grilled cheese sandwich could be salvaged.

"I can't believe you're eating that."

"A little dirt won't kill me."

"I'd do the same thing myself." She grinned. "Ten second rule applies as long as there's no hair stuck to it."

"Protein." He stuffed the last bite into his mouth. "We need to finish our book."

They sat beside each other on the sofa and listened

to the paranormal romance unfold. Before dinnertime, it had come to a happy conclusion. Liz let him help with dinner as long as he could do it from his seat at the bar.

"You're spoiling me. What will I do when you are gone away and I have to fend for myself?"

"I'm only spoiling you because you are not a hundred percent yet. When you're well, I'll sit on my round rear-end and let you cook for me."

Ian liked the idea. It sounded as if she planned to be around after he was mended. He hoped with all his might it would be so.

"Okay, favorite food?" He asked.

She answered and asked him the same. They went back and forth with the little game of Q & A until he knew many things about her, and she him. He thought a bottle of her favorite wine along with her favorite flowers might make a nice gift. He ventured to ask a daring question.

"How many kids do you want?"

She turned away, so he couldn't see her reaction. When she turned back to face him, she smiled, but it didn't hide the sorrow in her eyes.

"I can't have kids the old fashioned way...which is actually part of the reason why I'm divorced."

"Please don't tell me your ex-husband stepped out on you for that reason." His muscles tensed and he was surprised by the anger he felt toward a man he'd never met.

"I'm sorry. I shouldn't have said that. It's a long story."

"Do you feel comfortable sharing it with me?" *Please say yes.*

"It's a very uncomfortable subject for me. Historically, there's a stigma associated with barrenness."

"Yes, but culturally, haven't we evolved past that?"

"Not as far past it as you might think. I'm not sure if it's different because I grew up in the South, but most every little Southern girl *and* boy dreams of getting married and having kids when they grow up. Or maybe it's just expected."

"I suppose it's much the same where I'm from. Tell me what your fertility had to do with your divorce."

Liz rested her elbow on the bar and her chin on her fist while she thought. "I can't really tell you the whole story, but I'll tell you as much as I can."

"I don't mean to bring up unpleasant memories, Liz. I just want to understand."

She took a deep breath. "I was twenty-two when I married Jason. About a year later, he started making noise about wanting kids. I told him I wasn't ready because I wanted to finish my graduate degree, so we waited until then to try.

"After a year and a half with no success, I started seeing doctors and having every test imaginable to see what the problem was. Six years later, when I was about to get eggs harvested, he told me his girlfriend was pregnant." Her voice wavered.

"Bloody wanker." Ian didn't know what else to say. It was bad enough she was thrown off for another woman, but one who easily got pregnant while she struggled was a double blow.

She half smiled.

"Did the tests reveal anything conclusive?"

She shook her head and looked down at the counter.

"The best I can figure is endometriosis, possibly cervical stenosis. No one ever gave me a definitive diagnosis."

"I may play a doctor on TV, but that doesn't mean I comprehend what you're saying."

She covered her eyes with her hand for a moment before she looked up. He'd gone too far. She wasn't going to answer and she was going to leave him alone. His chest tightened with dread.

"Endometriosis is when uterine tissue grows outside the uterus. Cervical stenosis is when the cervix is very narrow and the swimmers have trouble getting through to reach the egg."

"But if you really wanted kids, you could still harvest the eggs and have en vitro or something?" He had no idea why he was pushing the issue.

"I suppose, but I'm getting older. I know women do it all the time, but there's a much greater risk for birth defects as maternal age increases. Plus, I'd need a sperm donor and I'd prefer him to be husband and father material, so I wouldn't have to raise a kid by myself."

He was the bloody wanker for speaking too soon. No way could he offer what she asked for.

"Don't look so terrified. After the divorce, I gave up the dream of having a family of my own and happily ever after. That only happens in fairy tales anyway." She turned her back to him and put her hands in the dishwater.

His brow furrowed and then he forced the wrinkle out. It bothered him that a woman with so much to offer, other than children, didn't think she could find happiness with a partner. It struck him that her infertility made them more compatible than he originally knew. Before he could think more of it, there was a knock at the back door.

Liz opened it to Danny. "Sorry, I forgot to text you. Dinner's ready, brother."

Danny placed a kiss on the top of Liz's head and walked in. "A man could starve to death waiting on you to call, Lizabelle. Hey, Ian, you look better than I expected."

"I swear if you find a woman who puts up with your BS, I am gonna beat it out of her."

"You put up with it, and you love me anyway."

"I wouldn't marry a man like you in a thousand years." She turned to Ian. "Danny has old-fashioned ideas about the roles of men and women."

"That's not entirely true." Danny sat on the stool next to him. "I just think there are some jobs more suited to men and others to women."

"Like, you prefer your woman in the kitchen," she said.

"Not necessarily. You're a good cook, so sue me if I'd rather eat your cooking than my own. But, when it comes to women in combat situations, I don't see any need for that."

"You're gonna meet your match one day and I'm gonna laugh my tail off when she puts you in your place." Liz set a plate in front of Danny.

"You two argue like real siblings," Ian interjected.

"I argue with Lizabelle like I do my brothers, except for my brothers and I wind up on the ground wrestling before it's over. My other sisters are sweet."

"You intimidate them, so they never challenge the great and mighty big brother." She placed a glass of water in front of Danny.

"Speaking of a challenge," Danny said. "I have an idea to run by you two."

"Let's hear it," Ian said.

"I think you should go home with Lizabelle after your appointment next week."

Ian thought for a moment and looked at Liz to gage her reaction. She shrugged and turned away to get Danny an extra napkin.

"I did plan to lay low until the swelling and bruising were completely diminished, but I don't want to impose on Liz."

"It wouldn't be an imposition," Liz said.

"Great," Danny said. "Make sure your doctor clears you to fly and I'll let my pilot know."

"Your pilot?" Ian asked.

"Company jet," Danny said around a mouthful of chicken.

Ian looked inquisitively at Liz, but she wasn't giving anything away. *Wealthy, indeed.* Although for his part, all private security companies might have jets, but he doubted it.

CHAPTER ELEVEN

By the time they were in the air, it was late afternoon Pacific Time. It would be after midnight when they landed in Atlanta which Liz thought was very good for sneaking a celebrity into her house.

Danny's plane was bigger than her dad's and she didn't get motion sickness as severely when she flew on the bigger planes. Rather than taking her medication, she tried pressure point wrist bands and they worked like a charm.

She was able to sit next to Ian on the sofa in the back of the plane and play the Q & A game. It was a struggle not to stare at his newly revealed face. There was only slight swelling and discoloration and for the most part, he looked the same. The surgeon said the change would take place slowly over the next few months.

After a few benign questions, she went for daring. "Okay, first kiss?"

"It was on set, during a scene."

She choked on her water. "No way."

He patted her back until she stopped coughing. "I was thirteen—tall, gangly, and awkward."

"I was like that at thirteen too, except for...you know?" She glanced down at her chest even as her face warmed.

"Let's talk about that instead." He grinned.

"No, get back to the kiss."

"It wasn't in the script, but the director suggested it. The girls name was Leslie and she was a year older than me but a bit shorter. I'd seen plenty of kisses and always wanted to try it, so I gave it my best shot."

"And?"

"Neither of us wanted to open our mouths, so we basically looked like two fish bouncing off each other's lips. It was horrid."

Liz laughed. "That's some imagery."

"We rehearsed a little and it got better." He propped his elbow on the back of the seat. "Now, tell me about your first kiss."

"Oh, gosh." Liz sighed and looked off into the way-back. "Chris Ross. I thought I was in love with that boy. We're from a small town and they used to have teen dances at the Community Center. Some of my friends were in love with Danny and Jason, who were friends with Chris."

"How old were you?"

"I was fourteen and the boys were fifteen. They were too cool to dance–although just between you and me and the fencepost, Danny is a great dancer. But anyway, the boys held up the wall. My friends convinced me we could rig a game of Spin the Bottle so we could all kiss the boy we liked. I told them it would have to be rigged because I refused to kiss my brother or Jason. They sent me to tell Danny, but it was Jason who talked them into it." Liz shook her head at the memory and wondered why she never asked Jason who he hoped to kiss that night.

"Anyway, it worked out that I got to kiss Chris. It would've been perfect if Danny and Jason hadn't been heckling us. I think Chris was a little worried about my dad, too. They don't call him Big Dan for nothing."

"Did you ever date him afterward?"

"Not in high school, but we went out a few times after my divorce." Liz closed her eyes at the memory of their short dating experience. On the last date, he told her he was moving to the west coast for a job. She'd wondered if he might have stayed if she hadn't acted like such an idiot every time he took her out.

She opened her eyes. "I've been meaning to ask you something. Your tattoo?"

He touched the spot. "Luck is always on my side."

Liz fell over laughing. "I've never met anyone as corny as me."

When they arrived at her house, she showed Ian to the guest room across the hall from her bedroom. They were both exhausted so they immediately went to bed. The next morning over coffee, they planned meals for the rest of the week so Liz could make a trip to the grocery store. Ian tried to give her his credit card, but she declined.

When she got back, he helped her unload the groceries. "I love your house. It's very quaint."

"That's another word for small."

"I wouldn't call it small, plus you don't need much space since it's just you."

Thanks for reminding me I'm single and always will be.

He kept talking. "You have three bedrooms, two baths, a small office, and an open concept living/kitchen/dining area. That doesn't include the basement garage where you have not one, but two autos, plus a music area and gym. I'd say you're doing quite well."

Liz bristled at Ian's assessment. She thought she lived very modestly considering, but to hear Ian tell it, she was well off. She was, but it wasn't anyone's business but her own.

"Did I say something wrong?"

She put on a smile she didn't feel. "No, you summed it up nicely. The house needed a lot of work when I bought it. My dad and brothers helped me get it done. That's why I'm so proficient with power tools."

"I did wonder about that. Do you have before-and-after pictures?"

She smiled a real smile and nodded. "Do you want to see?" She powered up her computer and opened her photo files to show him.

He looked at a picture of her doing sheetrock work and then at the wall. "Remarkable."

She looked like hell in the photo with drywall mud on her face and in her hair, but she didn't care. She was proud of the hard work she put into her house. Danny could moan about a woman doing a man's job, but when it came to Liz and her house, he shut his mouth and watched in awe.

Liz only had one television in her *quaint* house, so they watched the evening news before bed. Severe weather was moving in from the west.

"If the tornado siren goes off, we need to get to the

basement."

"Right...Does that happen often?"

"No, but as a tornado survivor, I don't take any chances."

He turned to face her from his position next to her on the couch. He smelled good and he was so close. She swallowed.

"Tell me about the tornado."

"We lived in Dunwoody in the spring of '98 when we were hit by an F-2 tornado. Jason was working, so I was home alone when it happened. I hunkered down in the bathtub while the storm ripped the roof off part of the house. It was terrifying. Now, when it thunders, I panic."

He took her hands in his. "I'm so sorry. Were you hurt?"

"Emotionally scarred for life, but physically unharmed. I was very blessed in that respect." Her flesh tingled. She'd been guarded by angels that night. Ones she never saw, but knew were there. Her journal held the story of the experience in its entirety, but only her mama's ears had ever heard it. Most people would not believe her or understand.

Later that night, Liz trembled in her bed as lightning flashed and thunder boomed. She squeezed her eyes shut and considered going to the basement to sleep whether or not the sirens sounded.

"Liz." Ian stood in her open doorway, wearing the usual–pajama bottoms and nothing more. "May I lay with you a while?"

"Sure." She must have scared him with her story.

He lay down on top of the covers next to her on the Queen-sized bed and took her hand in his. Her body jerked at the next clap of thunder. It was really close.

He tugged her arm. "Come here."

She didn't see a reason to argue. One of the hardest parts of surviving storms was doing it alone. She rested her head on his chest as he wrapped his arms around her and held her close. Concentrating on Ian's heartbeat, she forced herself not to jump when the sky roared again. It would be bad if she hit him in the face and ruined his new nose.

When the weather seemed to move away, he loosened his grip and rubbed her back in a soothing manner. A shiver rippled through her body and she knew she should move away, but she didn't want to. She hadn't been held in a very long time, so she focused on breathing and relaxing as her eyes grew heavy.

***

Ian awoke the next morning to music. He opened his eyes to find he'd fallen asleep in Liz's bed. She was on her side with her back to him. The covers were thrown back and her thigh length nightshirt was up around her waist. Her legs were mile-long fantastic and he fought the urge to slide closer and rest his hand on her hip.

She reached over to the nightstand and answered her phone. "Johnny, do you know what time it is?"

"Lizabelle." Johnny's voice filled the room, so Ian determined she must have put it on speaker-phone.

"I just wanted to check on my big sister after the storm last night. It was a doozie."

Ian heard a beep and the ceiling fan started turning. That explained why the room was so warm.

"Power just came back on," she said.

"Let me know if you have any downed limbs and I'll come take care of it for you."

"Thanks, brother."

"Nick wants to say hey."

"Hey, Aunt Lizabelle, I love you."

"Hey, my sweet boy, I love you more. What're you doing up so early?"

"I just woked up. Were you scared when it thundered?"

"Yeah, baby, I was scared."

"Next time, I'll come hold your hand, 'kay?"

Liz chuckled. "Okay, sweet thing, I'll remember that."

When she hung up the phone and rolled onto her back, she froze.

Ian almost faked sleep, but decided against it. "Good morning."

She smiled and started wriggling the hem of her gown down to cover her hips. "I hope you didn't get your eyes full."

"Not nearly." He made himself look at her face. "I'm glad to know Nick volunteered to hold your hand the next time it storms though."

"He's four and precious...and so are you. Thank you...for holding my hand during the storm."

"It was my pleasure." He meant it. He enjoyed having her in his arms and hoped it wouldn't be the last time.

"It looks like a rainy day to follow that *Rainy Night in Georgia*," she said.

"It was *The Night That the Lights Went Out in Georgia*." He dipped his chin.

"At least, we weren't on a *Midnight Train to*

Georgia."

He grinned. "I think I've got *Georgia on My Mind.*"

"*Sweet Georgia Brown,* we need to stop punning songs about Georgia." She cackled.

He pulled her to his side, the covers a barrier between them. "Rain is good for snuggling up and watching the telly. I've a favor to ask."

She tilted her head up and raised her eyebrows. Her face was close and he forgot his plan for a flash in time as he imagined pressing his lips to hers.

He blinked to clear his head. "You can say no, but I'd like you to watch *Trauma* and give me feedback on my performance. We can fast-forward through the racy bits."

"But...I don't know much about your craft."

"You must know bad acting when you see it. I value your opinion. I'd really like to know what you think, if you find my character believable."

"Since you asked so nicely, I'll do it, but I wouldn't do this for just anyone." She pulled the sheet up to her chest and sat up.

"I know. That's what makes me so special." He winked.

The first two seasons were available for viewing on the network website. The premiere for the third season was a few weeks away so it was too late to change anything about those episodes. But, if Liz offered tips, he could apply them to his future endeavors.

The first love scene from Season One, Episode One came on and he reached for the remote to fast-forward.

"No, if I'm going to be objective, I better watch it all."

"If you want to see me starkers, all you have to do

is ask."

Color rose in her cheeks as she chuckled. "I think I should get used to seeing you on screen first."

Ian observed Liz as she viewed episode after episode. She gave him honest feedback about the things that worked and the things that needed work. He agreed with everything she suggested. Before she said anything negative, she would always preface it, "It may be the way the writer's wrote it, but..." or "It could be the direction, but..." She even gave him tips on how to angle his body to better show off his...assets.

"I wish I would've met you long ago." He refilled her water glass.

She stretched. "Timing is everything."

At that moment, Ian's agent called and he excused himself to answer.

"Where are you?"

"On holiday. What's up, Will?"

"I've got good news. The casting director for the romantic comedy called and it's down to you and one other actor for the lead."

"Which actor?"

"Breck Stanton."

"Then, I don't stand a chance."

"Maybe you do. Stanton has turned down a few RomComs for action roles. If he says no, you're in. We need to generate some positive media buzz. Find a date for the premiere or I'll find one for you."

"I'd rather go stag, Will. Bryan and I agreed, unless you have a serious attachment, premieres are no place for dates."

"You need to reconsider. I'll talk to Bryan. Think

about single actresses or models. Make a list and I'll make something happen.

"I'll get back to you."

Ian tossed the phone on the bed. He wished he'd been cleared to exercise because the thing he wanted to do most was go downstairs and take out his frustrations on Liz's heavy bag. He knew having an agent for guidance was a good thing, but he sometimes felt coerced to do things he really didn't want to do.

He stayed in his room a while in order to calm down and think about the single women he knew. There was only one he wanted to consider and he was fairly certain her answer would be no.

That night, Liz fell asleep on the sofa watching the show. Ian considered carrying her to bed, but he didn't want to wake her and he wasn't supposed to lift heavy weights yet. Not that he thought she was heavy, but he could hear her scolding him already. He covered her with a blanket and leaned down to brush her hair back.

He placed a kiss on her forehead. "Pleasant dreams, love."

CHAPTER TWELVE

Liz spent all of Thursday watching the show, finishing the last one after dinner. Her butt was numb from sitting so long and her eyes were dried out. "Okay. I'm hooked. I can't wait for the next season."

"Only a few weeks to wait. I'm glad you enjoyed it." His smile was humble and sincere.

"It's not as smutty as I originally thought."

"The first few episodes were a bit excessive in that regard. To hook the viewers." He pretended to cast a fishing line at her.

She responded by making fish face and swimming toward him, complete with gills flapping near her head. He caught her and pulled her into a hug.

She hugged him back for a moment before she pulled away. Higher than average heart rates might be dangerous to her health, but not as dangerous as handsome actors who dreamed of greater stardom. "Danny hasn't called me with our flight time yet, but I'm going to start packing." Plus, she needed to floss the popcorn kernels out of her teeth. How many bags had they eaten anyway?

"Liz." She turned back to Ian and he took her hands

in his. "Thank you for everything. You've helped me in more ways than you could possibly know, beyond what you were hired to do."

"I've enjoyed having you."

"But...you haven't had me, yet." His blue eyes smoldered.

Liz nearly peed her pants. It was a total cheese-ball line and she bought it. He held her gaze and moved a hand to tuck an errant strand of hair behind her ear. *Lawd-a-mercy, he's gonna kiss me.* Popcorn kernels be darned. Her heart kicked into overdrive as heat from south of the Mason-Dixon Line rushed up her neck and into her cheeks.

Her phone rang. *Dang technology.* She blinked hard before stepping away from their intense moment to answer it.

"Danny says to be ready by noon."

"All right. Goodnight, Liz." He went to his room.

She tossed and turned and wished for another thunderstorm just to get Ian back in her bed.

***

The next morning after breakfast, Liz sat on the floor of her closet. She couldn't concentrate on packing the night before because all she wanted to do was go to Ian's bed and see if he felt the same attraction to her she felt for him. She stopped herself from getting up a half dozen times. He was still recovering from his procedure. Kissing and other related activities might be ill-advised.

In her defense, she had spent two solid days watching him in various stages of undress on a fifty inch LCD screen. It was her excuse as to why her hormones were surging and she saw him as an object of desire—like every other woman on the planet. Starved for romantic intimacy, she was cognizant that being in close quarters with Ian might be hazardous for her heart even if her loins loved it.

"Lizabelle." A familiar voice called out, making her chest squeeze.

"In here, Jase." She hoped Ian was hiding.

"Hey, gorgeous." Jason bent and kissed the top of her head. "Having trouble deciding what to wear?"

"Yeah, what're you doing here?"

"Ladies and gentlemen this is your captain speaking." He cupped his hand over his mouth and used his pilot announcer voice.

Jason flew corporate jets for big wig executives. It was a great gig because he had a flexible schedule and more job security than the commercial airlines offered.

"Quit playing." She popped his leg.

"I'm not playing. Danny called me last night, made me sign all his contracts. I'm going to fly you and your mystery guest to L.A. in your dad's jet. You and I are coming back Monday. Who is it anyway? Danny wouldn't say. Do you think she'll like me?" Jason wriggled his eyebrows.

"Um...I'm not sure you're their type. Come on, I'll introduce you."

Liz couldn't imagine what Danny had been thinking. Jason was going to be ticked off when he found out who her guest was.

Ian's door was closed. She knocked and as soon as he opened the door, his eyes fixed on Jason who looked back and forth between her and her guest.

"Danny hired you to hide a man? No way, he wouldn't do that."

"Um, Jason this is Ian. Ian, Jason. Danny hired him to fly us back to L.A. He signed all of the appropriate paperwork so we should be all good. He's very professional, right Jase?"

"Um, yeah."

"A pleasure." Ian extended his hand, but his tone was cool and his posture rigid.

Liz tensed because Jason took a long moment to let Ian's hand hang mid-air before he grasped it. Then, Liz worried the men might attempt to see who had the strongest grip. As she was about to reach out to separate them, Jason let go.

"I re-filed the flight plan to leave earlier. I hope you can be ready to go in half an hour. Lizabelle, take your meclizine now so it'll kick in by takeoff."

"I need to finish packing." She walked to the kitchen and he followed. "Do you want to drive my new truck?"

"Heck, yeah. It'll be my test drive." He gave her his crooked grin, which still did something to her insides.

"Good, it needs gas." She tossed him the keys and he left on the errand.

Liz went back into her closet and wondered if Ian would seek her out. She hated her red hair at moments like this. The mirror on her closet door revealed her face and neck had splotches in an unattractive shade of magenta.

"I thought you'd be packed already." Ian leaned against the doorjamb.

"Yeah, no." She tossed a pair of jeans into the suitcase.

"That's him then?"

She forced herself to meet his gaze. "Ian, I never

dreamed you'd meet my ex. I shouldn't have overshared like I did." She sighed and massaged her temples with her fingertips. "I'm going to kill Danny."

"It's fine, love." He reached out and stroked her cheek with his thumb. "Your secrets are safe with me. As far as he knows, I'm just a client you were hired to help."

She smiled. "Thank you. He can be jealous sometimes, so it'd be best if he didn't think we were too...friendly."

Ian opened his mouth to speak, but closed it. He nodded and left her standing in her closet with a sinking feeling in her chest. Their friendship had come to an abrupt end, if it could even be called a friendship. After all, she was his caregiver. She tried to figure out the moment it had become more, but it seemed like it had been more from the beginning.

On the way to the airport, Jason looked over at her. "Your dad's plane is smaller than Danny's, so your motion sickness will be worse."

"Jason." She cut her eyes to where Ian sat in the back seat and gave a small shake of her head reminding him not to say too much. "I know. I'm good and doped up."

"Jason, have you been flying long?" Ian asked.

Liz let out a long quiet breath, relieved because once Ian got the conversational ball rolling, Jason carried it. Ian needed only to offer a small reply or a new question to prevent a lull. Liz relaxed into the seat and closed her eyes. She had a lot to think about.

CHAPTER THIRTEEN

They boarded Liz's father's jet and Ian looked around. The Cessna was smaller than Danny's, but knowing Liz's family was wealthy enough to own and operate their own aircraft gave him food for thought. It was odd that Liz and Danny both lived rather modestly. He imagined Southland must be a very grand estate.

Jason entered the open cockpit and Ian and Liz settled in single seats across the aisle from each other. Liz played the part of detached caregiver well. He supposed he should concentrate on his part, but there was a hollow feeling in his chest he'd never had before. His hand rubbed the spot absently until he looked down and caught himself.

He wasn't prepared to give her up yet. He hadn't had enough time with her, but he would respect her wishes. Before he'd left her room earlier, he took her phone and programmed his number into it and texted himself. He smirked at his own cleverness.

Before takeoff, Jason came back and squatted next to Liz. "How you feelin', darlin'?"

"Sleepy. Just fly right. Don't make me sick on

purpose."

"Now why would I do that? You think I like holding your hair when you upchuck? Ian, if I were you, I'd move back a seat, just in case."

"I'm sure I'll be quite all right. If she turns green, I'll make a run for it."

"Smart man." Jason returned to the cockpit.

Ian didn't particularly care for Jason since he knew his history with Liz. He could be a male model since he stood just over six feet and was fit. He had dark blond hair, light brown eyes, and that easy charm women find so attractive.

Liz put her earbuds in and turned toward the window. She was asleep before they reached cruising altitude.

Jason put it on autopilot and looked back. "She can't handle drugs very well. It's the red-hair or something. She's more sensitive to stuff like that, although she used to put away some alcohol."

"You've known her a long time?" Ian feigned ignorance.

"Since before she became Danny's sister. I was gonna band together with him in a show of solidarity against Lizabelle, Katie, and Maddie, but they weaseled their way into our hearts."

"You're close to the family then?"

"I was very close to all of them." He gazed at Liz's sleeping form. "But life happened and I made some mistakes. We aren't as close as we used to be, but I'm working on it."

Jason sounded like he hoped for another chance with Liz. Ian didn't want that to ever happen.

"Are you married? Do you have children?" Ian

asked, aware he was pushing close to the edge of decency, but not caring.

Jason looked back at Ian. "Divorced, no kids. How 'bout you?"

Ian blanked for a second, wondering about the pregnant girlfriend. "Never been married. No children to speak of."

"I've seen your show. I bet you have to beat the women off with a stick."

"I haven't had to yet," Ian said, thinking he would never hit a woman with a stick. "I was in a serious relationship until the end of last year. It didn't work out, so I've been enjoying my single status for a bit."

"I bet you have. Good for you. My advice, get as much as you can before you get married then don't ever stray, no matter what."

"Spoken like a man with regrets."

"You have no idea." Jason cast a longing look at Liz before he turned back to the control panel.

Jason was still in love with her. Ian hadn't been sure what he wanted until he found out he might have competition. He was under the impression Danny wanted him to pursue his sister. He'd set up a rival and it worked. Ian wanted Liz more than ever. Whether Danny had done it on purpose or unwittingly, it was on, as they say.

When they began their descent into Los Angeles, Ian shook Liz's arm. She opened her eyes and blinked a few times. She looked at him for a moment before she smiled and removed her earbuds.

"We're about to land," he said, staring at her lips.

"The attendants on this bus suck. I didn't get beverage service and I have serious cottonmouth," she said as she stretched.

"You slept through it." Ian teased her as his eyes followed the length of her body.

Her smile wavered. She cut her eyes toward Jason and grimaced before she turned it back on. It was one of her best features, along with the eyes, the hair, the hips, the legs. He could keep going. It was the whole package he wanted.

When they landed, Danny was there to pick them up. Jason and Danny did a combination handshake/hug that men sometimes do before Jason climbed in the front seat with Danny, leaving Liz to sit in the back seat with Ian. She looked groggy and he was afraid she'd sleep all the way to his house.

"What are you gonna do now that you're pretty again?" Her voice was soft.

"I might get a leading role in a movie."

"Perfect. I bet a romantic comedy will shoot you over the moon."

"You think so?"

"Without a doubt." She held his stare and blinked slowly.

Ian was entranced and had nearly forgotten they weren't alone until Danny interrupted them.

"Ian, I don't know how your pantry looks since you've been away, but we're putting some steaks on the grill tonight and I've got one with your name on it. I hope you'll join us for supper."

"I'm salivating already. I'd be delighted to join you. May I bring something?"

"I've got it covered," Danny said.

"This might be the first time I've visited you, Danny, that you cooked for me," Liz said as she pumped her fist.

"I hate to break it to you, Lizabelle, but I was hoping you'd do the baked potatoes and salad."

"No problem, that's easy."

Danny dropped Ian at his house since he had luggage. He paused before he closed the car door and gave Liz a wink. "See you in a bit."

***

Liz didn't even try to hide her smile when Ian arrived with a bouquet of flowers and a bottle of her favorite wine. Jason followed Ian in from outside.

"This is to thank you for your hospitality." Ian kissed her cheek.

"All you had to get her was a six pack and she would've been happy," Jason said.

She ignored Jason. "I love this wine. Thank you, Ian. You shouldn't have."

"But you're glad he did, right, Lizabelle?" Jason said and she stifled a growl. Her ex apparently wanted it known that he was familiar with her habits, even though she didn't drink much anymore.

Liz could tell by Ian's eye roll how annoyed he was by Jason's presence.

She handed Jason two beers from the fridge for him and Danny and he went back outside while Liz poured two glasses of wine. "Sorry about that."

"Not your fault. Surely your brother didn't intend to be cruel."

"No, he was desperate. My dad's pilot..." She stopped abruptly then realized it was too late, Ian already knew her dad and brother had their own jets. He didn't have to know they were gifts from her. "He had an emergency and the back-up was in a wedding.

Jason was third string."

"The Bakers are real jet-setters then."

Liz felt her cheeks warm as she looked down at the floor. "Not really, we're just regular people."

Ian took her hand. "It's nothing to be ashamed of."

She wasn't ashamed, but she did feel money was a personal matter. "I know, but sometimes people treat you differently if they know. We just try to live simple lives, Ian, and do what we can to help others."

"Your humility is very becoming."

"Sounds like a load." She smirked. "Stop it and help me with this salad. Here, chop something." She pushed a knife, cutting board and a tomato toward him.

He obliged and they settled into an easy conversation while they worked. Over dinner, they sat next to each other and across from Danny and Jason, but didn't talk much.

"Hey, Ian, have you heard Danny and Lizabelle play?" Jason asked.

"Liz is extremely talented. My favorite musician, in fact. Bryan's too." Ian leaned into her and bumped her shoulder. "I haven't had the pleasure of hearing Danny play."

"Bryan Watson? No way!" Jason said. "I can't believe you guys met him. He seems like someone I'd like to hang out with."

"He *is* like someone you'd hang out with." Danny wiped his mouth. "Nice guy. Liz taught him to two-step."

"You're joshin' me!"

Liz was annoyed with Jason's exuberance over Bryan. If Jason had met Ian under different circumstances, he would've reacted similarly.

After dinner, Jason insisted they play something for Ian. Liz was still shy about singing in front of him, but not doing it would draw speculation from both Jason and Danny. Her brother was probably fully aware of her feelings without her having to say anything at all.

She was quick to make song suggestions where Jason could sing and she and Danny could add harmony. Ian took the seat next to her on one of the couches and the boys sat across on the other couch.

"Feel free to sing along, Ian, if you know these songs," Jason said.

To Liz's surprise, Ian did join them on a chorus of a Crosby, Stills, Nash, and Young song. Of course, he sounded great. She stopped playing for a beat and looked at him. When he turned her way, she jumped back in.

"Whew, that sounded good, man," Jason said.

"Musical theater," Ian said.

"What's another one with tight harmony we can do?" Danny asked.

"Seven Bridges Road," Liz said.

"Hell, yeah," Jason said. "Sorry Liz, baby, you know how I am when I get excited."

Liz felt her brows pinch together. *Did he just call me baby?* Before she could set him straight on the matter, Jason pitched them in and they sang the song. It was a good thing Ian was a fan of Southern rock.

"We should take this show on the road." Danny was excited, too. She liked seeing her brother happy and when he and Jason were together, they always had fun.

"What else?" Jason asked.

"One more, then I'm hitting the hay." She yawned. "Especially, if you expect me to help haul the old deck to the dump tomorrow."

"I need you to cut 'em down. We'll haul 'em," Danny said. "Let's do one by the Indigo girls so you can sing lead, Lizabelle."

"Uh, Danny, I like the high part."

"Jason can sing the high part." Danny stared her down.

He was trying to show her off to Ian. She shook her head at her brother.

"I'm not certain I know the lyrics to their songs," Ian said.

"We should sing something by the Doobie Brothers," she offered.

"Yeah, yeah, yeah." Jason launched into a song.

Liz smiled at Danny as they joined their voices with Jason and Ian. She needed to figure out what Danny was up to. He played innocent, but she knew he had a lot of Big Daddy in him. Their dad could manipulate folks like pieces on a chessboard.

Liz put her guitar away and was surprised when Ian took the case from her and propped it against a wall. "Walk me out."

She followed and thanked him again for the flowers and wine and for sharing his voice with them. He took her hands and pulled her toward him. She anticipated his lips. When they were so close she could feel the heat from them, the back door opened and she levitated three feet backward, like an idiot.

Jason stood in the doorway. "You okay, Lizabelle?"

"Yes. Goodnight, Ian." She walked, shamefaced, right past Jason, into the house, and into her room where she screamed into her pillow.

CHAPTER FOURTEEN

Ian was still waking up when he staggered into Danny's backyard the next morning. Sleep hadn't come easily as he speculated over Liz's reaction to their almost kiss getting interrupted by her ex-husband. It had to be difficult for her to be friends with him and Ian couldn't wrap his head around it.

"Mornin'," Danny said. "Thanks for helping out."

Liz came out the back door with a coffee mug in hand. She was dressed similarly to the way she'd been the first day he met her. Because she had long legs, normal length shorts looked short on her, but Ian wasn't going to complain. They were lovely.

"If you can peel your eyeballs off my sister's legs, there's coffee inside."

After they each finished a cuppa, they got to work. Danny backed his truck up for easy access. Liz came out carrying an extension cord and a small saw. Ian watched her prepare to work and was surprised when Jason sidled up next to him.

"They're nice, aren't they? They go on for miles, especially in high heels."

Ian cleared his throat. "Ah, yes, right you are."

He decided not to pretend he wasn't looking. Liz was a beautiful woman. He was certain he wasn't the first man to admire her, nor would he be the last.

Liz cut the deck boards while the men carried the lumber and loaded it in the truck. The bed filled quickly and it became evident they would have to make two trips. They got into Danny's truck, Danny and Jason in front, he and Liz in the back seat and began their journey.

Danny said, "Jase, help me look for a road named Mary something."

"Are you trying to tick your sister off?" Jason asked.

"What?" Liz asked.

"Nothing," Danny said. "Nothing to see here, enjoy your eye candy in the back seat.

"Is he speaking about you?" Ian asked Liz.

"No, I think he's talking about you."

"You're the only eye candy I see in here," Ian said.

"Well, I've got three pieces of eye candy. I win." She grinned.

Half an hour into the journey, Liz asked, "Danny, are you lost?"

"As a goose."

She thumped the back of his head.

"Ow, Lizabelle, that doesn't help."

"For a man who was trained to get out of a jungle with a pack of matches and a roll of duct tape, you sure are directionally challenged sometimes," Liz said. "It's a good thing you have GPS."

"I can't work this thing. And if any of you tell anyone, I'll make sure you come to a painful end."

"See." Liz leaned to whisper to Ian. "Everyone

struggles with inadequacies sometimes."

He rested his hand on her back, glad they could share a private moment.

"Your sister's a freaking computer genius and you can't work the GPS?" Jason said. "Oh, I forgot for a second you aren't blood kin."

"Actually, it's more like my brother doesn't want *Big Brother* tracking his every move." Liz pulled out her cell phone, found the landfill on the map and directed Danny to it.

"You'll have to excuse her, Ian." Jason turned in his seat. "Getting lost is one of her pet peeves and Danny and I are good at it."

"They do it just to aggravate me." She smirked.

"Settle down, sister."

"Don't make me thump you again. We've been wasting time. We have another load and didn't you say the landfill closes at noon today?"

"Oh shoot, I forgot."

Ian was being entertained while learning something new about Liz. The return trip took only fifteen minutes, but they didn't have any time to waste. Liz bent to cut the remaining deck boards. Ian paused, impressed by her use of the saw.

It was late May and the day was clear and unseasonably hot. He stripped his t-shirt off before it was soaked through with sweat. Liz wore a long-sleeved fishing shirt, which was supposed to keep the wearer cooler and protect them from the sun's harmful rays. It clung to her skin, soaked with perspiration.

Ian walked toward her to get the last boards after she made the final cut. She stood and shook her legs, then swayed on her feet. She dropped the saw and moved to hold onto the side of the truck, but Ian got to her first. He carried her into the garage and put her in a folding chair. An industrial size fan was close by, so he aimed it in her direction. He expected Danny or Jason to come in at any moment, but apparently they hadn't seen her almost faint. If they had, they would have shoved him aside.

"Will you be all right a moment while I get you some cold water?"

She nodded, but her eyes were glazed and stared at nothing.

Ian rushed inside and out at record speed. She'd taken her hat off and her hair was plastered to her head. He knelt beside her with an open bottle of water and poured some of it onto paper towels before putting the bottle in her hand. While she drank, he placed one of the cold, wet towels on her throat and the other on her forehead.

"Better?" He asked when she'd downed half of the liquid.

He moved one of the towels to the back of her neck. She closed her eyes for a moment and he held onto her for fear she would fall over.

"Are you two ready to go?" Danny asked.

Liz opened her eyes and squinted at her brother.

"I think she rose too quickly and got dizzy." Ian moved the towel around to the front again.

"You're red as a beet, sis." He knelt in front of her. "You gonna be alright?"

She cleared her throat. "Yeah, I just got overheated."

"I'll stay here with her, mate, if you and Jason want to make the last trip." Ian was trying to remind him the landfill would close soon.

"I appreciate it, man, but I don't want to leave her if she's gonna pass out."

"I won't. I'm already feeling better. I'll go drink some Gatorade and sit in the air conditioning."

"I'll call 911 if she passes out." Ian hoped it wouldn't come to that.

"I'm *not* going to pass out." The *not* was the only word which didn't sound weak.

"Call me if you need me." Danny squeezed her shoulder. "I'm not going to mention this to Jason. He'll get...concerned."

Liz waved her hand at Danny, and then leaned down to take her work boots off.

"Allow me." Ian was still kneeling next to her and pushed her upright.

He removed her shoes and socks while she used the wet paper towels to wipe her face and neck. His throat constricted and he realized he needed to take control of the situation, and his emotions.

"My head is on fire, literally." She giggled and Ian grew more concerned.

"Let's get you inside where it's cooler."

He moved to pick her up and she swatted at him. "Let me walk. You haven't been cleared for heavy lifting."

"You're *not* heavy, love." He put his arm around her waist and helped her inside.

He set her on a chair at the bar before he got a bottle of Gatorade. While she drank, he wet a clean cloth with cool water and put it on the back of her neck. "You frightened me. I thought you were going down."

"So did I."

"Your face is still quite red. Come with me, I've an idea."

He pulled her to the bathroom and turned the shower to cold. He started unbuttoning her shirt, but she put her hands up to stop him.

"You're wearing something under here, right?"

She nodded and dropped her hands so he could proceed. She wore a sport bra underneath. He would've liked to take more time to admire her, but she wasn't well. He removed his shoes and helped her into the shower. She closed her eyes as the cold water washed over her head. He hoped it would immediately do its task of cooling her down.

"I'm a real hothead."

"You're either feeling better or getting delirious. Have you eaten solid food today?"

She shook her head and propped a forearm on the tiled shower wall. "I didn't think cutting and hauling the old lumber away would take so long."

Ian picked up the shampoo bottle and smiled. Her eyes popped open when she heard the cap do the same.

"As long as I'm here, I might as well return the favor."

She leaned her head back into his hands as he worked the shampoo into her hair. By the time he helped rinse the conditioner from her hair, she had chills. Whether it was from the cold water or his hands, he couldn't be sure.

"Can you take it from here?"

"Yes, thank you."

"I'll be right outside if you need me."

Before he left the bathroom he got a towel for

himself and laid one out for her. In the hallway, Ian removed his soaked shorts and dried himself as he carried his wet clothes outside. He left the towel wrapped around his waist and waited outside the bathroom door.

He was glad he noticed her stumble a bit and got to her before she fainted. It had been a vexing moment for him, to see her in distress. He cared more deeply for her than he wanted to admit.

When the door opened to the bath, he stood in front of her to make certain she was steady. He was momentarily distracted by the sight of her wrapped in a towel. Blinking, he took her by the arm and escorted her to her room.

"You dress. I'll find something to eat."

"Thank you."

He made peanut butter sandwiches for them both, grabbed two bottles of water and napkins and returned to her room. She was lying on her bed, propped up on pillows. She donned cutoff sweats and a loose T-shirt. He climbed atop the bed and sat next to her, trying to keep his towel from coming unraveled. He gave her a sandwich which she obediently ate.

"My head is pounding. I think I'll take a nap and see if it goes away."

"Come nap at my place. I'll keep an eye on you while Danny and Jason hang out."

"You're very sweet, but I don't want to impose."

"It's no imposition. I want to take care of you for a change."

Her smile was weak. "Let me text Danny real fast."

"While you do that, I'll run home to get trousers. I'll be back to get you straight away."

On his way back, Ian found Liz walking to his house on her own.

"Oh no, you don't." He picked her up.

"Ian, you aren't supposed to lift things yet. I can walk."

"I just got you cooled down. There's no need to get overheated again."

"I think there's still a fair chance for that to happen as long as you're holding me." She gasped and covered her mouth with her hand.

He tried not to grin like an idiot.

"I'm sorry, something is wrong with my filter."

"Filter?" He asked.

"Yeah, the thing you run ideas through before you let them come out of your mouth."

"I see." He was still grinning when he carried her to his bed and laid her on it.

"No, Ian, I really will be imposing if I take over your bed. Put me in the guest room."

"No can do, love. There's no telly in the guest room and I intend to keep an eye on you. Go ahead and rest here while I grab a quick shower." He gave her the controller to adjust the bed.

He remembered the cold compresses she used on his eyes and got one for her before he went into the bath. When he exited the bathroom, she was asleep.

***

Liz opened her eyes and smiled at Ian who was seated next to her on the bed.

He leaned over her. "How are you feeling?"

"Not sure yet."

"Danny will be here in a moment. Can I get you anything?"

She looked around and saw it was dark outside. "That was a long nap." She sat up and moaned at the pounding in her head. "Bad idea."

Ian raised the head of the bed and then held her up while he piled pillows beneath her back. "Is it your head? Would you care for an aspirin?"

"There's a drum line performing in my frontal lobe. Do you have anything for a migraine? I'm afraid aspirin won't cut it."

"Never fear, Lizabelle." Danny walked into the room with her toiletry bag in hand. "I've got you covered." He pulled out a pill bottle and handed it to her.

"I'll get water." Ian left the room.

"Well, look at you, propped up in Ian Clarke's bed." Danny crossed his arms over his chest.

"Like this wasn't your end game."

"I don't know what you mean." He held his hands out, palms up.

"You're too smart to play dumb with me, bro."

He pushed her over and sat next to her on the bed. "Seriously though, are you okay staying here?"

"Yes, Ian's taking good care of me."

"I'm glad you think so," Ian said, coming back into the room.

"I can't stay long. Jason was in the shower when I left. We're going out to eat and to the Rusty Roof. I'll keep him out late so he won't realize you're not there. I told him I convinced Ian to entertain you so he and I can have guy's night out."

"Go on then. Have fun." She took the migraine medicine and pressed her fingertips to her temples to relieve the pressure in her head.

"Do you feel like eating?" Ian asked after Danny left.

"No way." She had the nausea which often accompanied migraines. "I'm just going to close my eyes for a minute."

The next time Liz opened her eyes, it was daytime. The medicine knocked her out. She moved her head from side to side. The intense pain was gone and only a dull ache remained.

Ian was sleeping beside her, miles away on the other side of the bed. Her bladder was about to burst, but she didn't want to wake him. She struggled with what to do and at last, her bladder won the argument.

She sat up slowly and eased off the bed. She looked down at her rumpled t-shirt and shorts as she went into the bathroom and closed the door. She almost peed herself at the sight of her hair. She had fallen asleep with it wet and now it looked like a family of squirrels had moved in and nested. *Bladder first, hair later.*

When she washed her hands, she used handfuls of water to smooth her hair down. She needed a brush, but hers was missing from her toiletry bag. She didn't want to plunder through Ian's bathroom drawers, but decided a quick peek wouldn't hurt. The first drawer she opened contained oral hygiene implements. The next held shaving cream and other manly grooming gadgets. There was a comb that was certain to get trapped in her tangles, but no brush.

She gave up the search and decided her best bet would be to wet her hair in the sink and start over. She didn't think through the consequences of her actions and before her hair was even half wet, the intense throbbing pain returned. She closed her eyes to hold back the tears as the little drummer boy played a song in her skull.

She abandoned her goal of hair repair and returned to an upright position. Sitting on the edge of the tub, she towel-dried her hair and finger-combed it a little before abandoning the task with a sigh. It occurred to her she should be embarrassed Ian would know she wanted to fix her hair for him. She was midway to standing when Ian knocked on the door.

"Liz, are you all right?"

She was startled by his knock and she leaned back with a jerk, lost her balance and landed on her butt in the bathtub. Thankfully, she didn't hit her already devastated head, but she might have bruised her coccyx. The towel thoughtfully cushioned the blow.

"Ouch!" Her eyes overflowed with tears.

The door banged open and Ian rushed in. She covered her face with part of the damp towel.

"What happened, love? Where are you hurt?"

"I fell." She sobbed, sounding like a little kid.

She didn't realize he'd stepped into the tub with her until he was picking her up. "If you want a bath, you need only ask and I'll oblige."

He laid her on the bed, pulled the towel away from her face and smoothed her hair back. She was an ugly crier. Her face scrunched up and she turned red and stayed red. She smoothed out her face, but the tears kept falling out of her eyes and into her ears.

Ian swiped at the first few then used the towel to block the path leading to her ears. He leaned down and kissed her forehead and she didn't feel like crying anymore.

"Would you care to tell me how you wound up

falling into the bath?"

She explained what happened with one slight embellishment. Her reason for wetting her hair was because it was tangled and she had no brush. She couldn't very well say, "I didn't want you to see me with ratty, bed-head." Although now that she looked, he had a little bed-head going on, too. But he still looked good; bed-head was cute on him.

He went into the bathroom and returned with a brush. She wondered where it'd been hiding? Ian positioned pillows in her lap and had her sit up and lean forward a bit while he slid in behind her. He took small sections of her hair and began to work the brush through them very gently until the tangles were gone. He'd done it before, because he knew how to create slack at the scalp when he needed to force the brush through so it wouldn't pull and hurt.

She closed her eyes. "Who've you been practicing on?"

"I have three sisters. They all had long hair when we were children. The youngest, Sylvie, was extremely tender headed and Mum would lose patience while trying to comb out her hair. Sylvie would cry when she saw a hairbrush, which is probably the reason she has short hair today."

Liz smiled at the affection in his voice as he spoke about his sister.

"When Mum would get impatient with Sylvie, I'd take over and because I felt so sorry for her, I'd spend what seemed like hours working the brush through the tangles. I'm sure it was hours because it felt as if my arms might fall off before I completed the task."

"Well, I don't want your arms to fall off. I'm not

usually very tender-headed, in fact, most people would say I'm hard-headed, but I do appreciate your gentle touch, especially with this headache."

He swept her hair over to one side and his lips pressed a light kiss on the curve of her shoulder. Shivers ran through her. He then separated her hair into two sections and braided each one.

"Now when you sleep, it shouldn't get so tangled. Slide down and lie back."

He placed pillows in his lap and she did as he commanded. He gave her the world's greatest head massage. Liz always got relief from her headaches with pressure points. Her mom used to do it for her when she still lived at home. She closed her eyes as he lightly pinched along her brow bones. *Lord, can I keep him*?

CHAPTER FIFTEEN

Ian continued to massage Liz's head until she was asleep again. He needed to feed her the next time she awoke. Perhaps caffeine would improve her headache. He brushed his fingers lightly across her brow. He was completely taken with her and wondered if there was a way he could hope to keep her.

She lived in Atlanta, near her family, but Danny said she could work from anywhere. He didn't think she'd be at all interested in his celebrity lifestyle. She'd said playing in a band at a low-key country bar was as big as she wanted her spotlight to get. He knew it would be asking a lot, but he wanted to test the waters, see if she was willing. Would she think he was worth the effort?

Ian was watching the telly with the sound barely audible when he glanced down to see Liz studying his face. He hoped his nose didn't still look swollen from her vantage point. The sleepy smile she flashed nearly stole his breath. He envisioned a lifetime of waking up with her.

"How do you feel?" He asked.

"Better, I think."

She started to rise, but he slipped his arms beneath hers and pulled her up and back against his chest. Wrapping his arms around her, he kissed the side of her head. "How about now that you're upright?"

She didn't answer right away so he leaned around to see her face. She was still smiling and she raised her eyebrows at him.

She gave a little nod of her head. "No drummers in there. I think the worst has passed. Thank you so much for seeing about me."

"My pleasure. I'll get you something to eat in a moment, but I'd like to ask you something first."

She leaned and turned her head a little more toward him.

"Will you accompany me to the premiere of my show?"

Her smile fell from her face and her eyes widened. "Do you mean...um...red carpet and cameras?"

"There will be a red carpet and lots of cameras, also, lots of fans and press. There's a big party afterward. You said you looked forward to the next season, this is chance to see the premiere." He was trying to think of every positive thing to say about it.

"I don't know, Ian. I'm a disaster lately, I might embarrass you. I can see the headlines now, Ian Clarke's date trips in her high-heels and face-plants in the middle of the red carpet. Dress covers her head, she wears Wonder Woman underwear."

"Now, you're just being silly." He chuckled at her runaway imagination. "I won't let you fall. Perhaps a fitted skirt is in order in the event of a strong wind, so you can still wear your Wonder Woman knickers."

He felt rather than heard her laugh as her body

shook in his arms.

"When is this shindig?"

"Two weeks."

"That's not enough time for me to lose ten pounds."

"Liz Baker, look at me." She did. "You do not need to lose any weight at all. If you do, I will disinvite you. Please don't fret over such things. You're beautiful just as you are."

"Ian–" she began, but stopped when his phone rang.

He flashed the display at her before he answered. "Mum."

"Darling, how are you?"

"Very well. I have another follow up tomorrow then I should be cleared for business as usual."

"Wonderful, and are you pleased with your result thus far?"

"Yes, Ma'am. It will take time, but I'm delighted. I can breathe and I look more like myself. In other news, Liz is here with me and she hasn't been feeling well this weekend."

"Oh dear, is she pregnant?" Her tone held a mixture of distress and excitement.

Ian was glad Liz hadn't heard that. "No, Ma'am, it isn't like that. It was heat exhaustion which developed into a migraine."

"Oh, the poor dear."

"I was just trying to convince her to escort me to the premiere, but she has many objections."

"Why would she object to stepping out with you? Unfathomable!" His mother was his biggest fan.

"Mum, do you recall what it was like when you attended your first premiere with father?"

"I do, put Elizabeth on the phone."

He put the phone against his chest. "Mum wants to speak to you. Shall I put her on speaker?"

"You're gonna gang up on me, huh?" She winked and he held the phone so she could press the speaker button. "Hi, Mrs. Clarke."

"Please, call me Jacqueline. Now, I know the idea of attending a premiere seems daunting, but it's a wonderful opportunity to get dressed up and celebrate with Ian. I hope you'll consider escorting him."

"Um...I'll consider it, but I haven't had a chance to really think it through. He sprung it on me a moment before you called."

"Tell me, what is your biggest objection?"

"Um...the first one that comes to mind is the size of my rump roast. I'm not a size zero like the rest of the women who live and work in L.A."

Ian narrowed his eyes and leaned so she could see him.

"Darling, you will be next to Ian. He makes any size woman look small."

"You have a point," Liz said.

"Thank you, Mum."

"What else?" His mum asked.

"I'm afraid I'll embarrass him. I'm just a plain country girl. I wouldn't know how to behave at a Hollywood premiere."

"Darling, Ian would not have invited you if he thought you would embarrass him. Just be yourself and have someone style your hair and make-up. Ian can connect you with a stylist. Take his credit card and go buy a lovely dress and accessories."

"Um...I have a stylist and access to dresses and accessories, so that's not a concern really."

"Well, the matter sounds quite settled. Liz, you should come visit us when Ian comes home after the premiere."

Liz didn't say anything and at her stunned look, Ian told his mum goodbye.

He wrapped his arms around her again. "Are you going to give in and say yes?"

"I need to make a few calls. Can I let you know by tonight?"

"Of course, now let's get lunch so I can fatten you up a bit." He patted her hips.

"Not funny."

***

Ian entered the back door at Danny's house and found Liz taking a dish out of the oven. She pressed her lips together and he hoped it was because she had good news and not because Jason was seated at the bar with Danny.

He couldn't wait to talk to her, but he didn't want to do it in front of her ex. She'd texted him that since she got back from Ian's house after lunch, Jason had been on her case. He didn't believe her story about falling asleep on the couch watching a movie. She wanted to make sure Danny and Ian were aware of the lie, too. Ian thought they should tell Jason it was none of his business what Liz did or why, but she admitted she preferred to avoid confrontation.

Jason's eyes were on her as she offered, poured, and delivered a glass of wine to Ian. "Since when do you prefer wine to beer, Lizabelle?"

She sighed. "Chris Ross introduced me to this particular wine a few years ago. It's addicting so I don't keep it on hand or I'd be an alcoholic."

"When did you see Chris Ross?" Jason asked.

"Come on, Jase, you know Lizabelle always had a crush on him." Danny sipped his beer.

"I do know, that's why I'm asking."

"How long ago did you date him?" Danny asked.

"You dated him?" Jason asked, chin down, eyebrows up.

"Dating is a strong word for what we did," Liz said.

"You slept with him?" Jason's eyebrows could no longer be seen under the fringe of hair on his forehead.

"No, you jerk. Not that it's any of your business." Liz's eyes were narrowed and her fists clenched.

Jason dropped his head in defeat and Ian refrained from cheering.

"They would've probably kept dating if Chris hadn't moved to Seattle." Danny might've been rubbing it in.

Ian couldn't figure out Danny's angle and he was tired of Jason's tirade. He wanted Liz's answer. "Do you have news for me?"

"Well, just put it out there, why don't cha?" She smirked at Ian and pressed her lips together. "Yes."

"Yes...is...your answer?" His eyebrows climbed northward as he spoke, but he returned them to their proper place.

"Yes."

He picked her up in a hug, unable to hide his excitement.

"Answer to what?" Jason asked.

"I'm still freaking out a little, but Ian invited me to the premiere of his show in a couple weeks and I'm going."

"Did you call Clay?" Danny asked.

"Yeah, and get this, he told me he still had my

measurements on file. I 'bout wet myself laughing."

"Who's Clay?" Ian asked.

"An evening wear designer in Atlanta. He designed all of Katie's pageant dresses and Liz used to model for him." Danny looked proud.

"Liz, I'm gobsmacked," Ian said. "You behave as though you've never been in the public eye."

She shuffled her feet and looked down. "That was a lot smaller scale than your premiere. I only did print and local runway shows and it was more than twenty years ago."

Ian stopped fretting so much over her tripping on the red carpet. Although, when he thought about it, he did seem to pick her up quite often.

He shook his head to clear it. "Hair and make-up is in order then?"

"If I let anyone other than Katie touch me, she'll have a fit. She's going to fly back out here with me for the weekend to make me glamorous. I hope that's okay, Danny."

"Perfectly fine. It'll be good to see Queenie."

By the time they finished dinner, Ian and Liz had decided on what color they thought would best compliment his charcoal gray suit which was being tailor made for him.

"Does my dress need to be long or short?"

"Either, you'll see both."

"Good, my legs are one of my best features."

"You got that right," Jason said before Ian could get the words out.

She ignored Jason. "Hopefully, Clay will come up with a design to hide my flaws and enhance my assets."

Ian looked forward to seeing more of those. Before he left, he hugged her goodbye, kissed her cheek and promised to call. He would've preferred a goodbye kiss on the lips, but since they had an audience, it would wait until another time. *Bloody Jason.*

CHAPTER SIXTEEN

Liz watched Ian leave and enjoyed the lingering sensation of tingling from his touch.

As soon as Ian was out of sight, Jason let her have it. "Have you lost your damn mind?"

"Jason, it's not your place." Danny sounded scary when he used his serious voice. "You had your chance. You blew it. Your time is over."

"Can't you just be excited for me? I get to dress up and have a glamorous night out in Hollywood."

"I don't begrudge you a Cinderella at the ball evening, but fairy tales end, Lizabelle. What about the expectations then? I don't want to see you get hurt. We may not be married anymore, but I still love you and want to protect you."

His words made Liz take a step back and Danny gave them privacy. Jason sounded sincere in his concern for her.

"I don't appreciate your interest in my personal life. I'm a big girl and I don't need you to protect me. I want this. It's just one night, then I'll go back to Atlanta and my ordinary life." Pressure was building behind her eyes and she didn't want Jason see her cry, so she tried to walk away.

He caught her arm. "Liz, he's not right for you. I am. You and me, we belong together. We can have a life together."

"I can't give you the life you want Jason." She didn't meet his eyes.

"What're you talking about? Kids? It probably didn't happen because I was putting too much pressure on you."

A tear slid out of the corner of her eye.

Jason wiped it away with his thumb. "We can see doctors again, if we need to."

"Once upon a time, I would've done anything to give you what you wanted, but I'm not willing to put myself through that now." She reclaimed her hands and wiped her eyes.

It was his turn to look ashamed. "I know I ruined what we had, but I want to regain your trust. We've rebuilt a friendship the last few years. I wish we could start again."

Liz dropped her head and rested the top of it on his chest. He was so warm and so familiar. His words tugged at her heartstrings. She didn't doubt he loved her. It would be so easy to fall back into his arms, but she couldn't. If he hurt her again like before, she'd never get over it. She'd barely recovered the first time and it was still a struggle, especially when she let herself feel the betrayal again. She released the barrier keeping those emotions contained in her mind. It was a good thing they came back so fiercely; otherwise, she might repeat her mistakes. She wasn't perfect, but some mistakes couldn't bear repeating.

"You have to let us go." She looked him in the eyes

even though her voice was shaky.

His jaw clenched and his hands fisted. "Ian is going to hurt you. He's gonna play with your heart and then toss you aside."

"I should be prepared for it then, 'cause I already know how that feels."

He flinched as if her words struck him with a physical blow.

"Why wasn't I enough for you, Jason?" The tears fell unbidden.

He put his arms around her, pulled her close and kissed the side of her head. "You were, but I was too stupid to realize it. You're the best thing that ever happened to me, you're the best part of me. I know you'll never be able to trust me, but I want to be a man who is worthy of the love of a woman like you."

"You already are worthy of love, but you've been holding on to regret for too long. Forgive yourself so you can breathe again. There's a lucky woman out there waiting for you to get it together."

He held her face in his hands. "You're sure it can't be you?"

She shook her head and wiped at her eyes. "I'll always love you, Jason, but I can't put my heart in your hands again. I'm sorry."

He nodded and blinked back tears of his own. "I really do want you to be happy, Lizabelle. If Ian can do that for you, then I wish you all the love in the world." He kissed her lips very lightly and left her there.

She went to her room and allowed herself to mourn Jason once again. After a knock at the door, Danny came in and sat next to her on the bed.

"That talk was a long time coming." He put an arm around her. "You okay?"

She nodded as she pulled her knees to her chest and hugged them. "Maybe we can both move on now."

"Have you thought about how going to premiere will make you a target for curiosity seekers? I only mention it because you and I both like to keep our cards close to the vest. Are you prepared for everyone to find out about you?"

"I hadn't thought it through. It won't be easy for them to trace anything back to me because of my name changes and the DBA and the LLC."

"Let's see, you were a Johnson before we adopted you, then a Baker, then you married Jason and became a Powell, divorced him and went back to Baker. What is your legal last name now anyway?"

She elbowed him lightly in the ribs. "I'll always be a Baker, but I do business as Johnson with my Limited Liability Company, Southland States. I told you it was complicated."

"Did Dad help you figure all that out?"

She nodded. "And Aunt Nancy. Big Daddy's got the business brain and Aunt Nancy's got the legal stuff covered. It's not impossible to find out about me, but it's not easy either."

"Have you and Ian talked about what happens after the premiere?"

"No, I don't want to plan past it. He probably only asked me to see if I could handle the pressure of Hollywood. It'll be a miracle if I survive it, but I don't want that lifestyle and I would never ask him to give it up. It's not serious between us, it's not like we're in love. We're just friends."

"Uh-huh." Danny stood but before he left, he put his hand over his heart. "Protect yourself."

She took a moment to be sad at the thought of losing Ian after the premiere. It was a ridiculous thought, because you can't lose something you don't have.

The melancholy didn't last long because the excitement of getting ready for the premiere soon pushed it away. Ian was going to look H-O-T, so she needed to schedule tanning, waxing, facials, hair treatment, and teeth whitening in between fittings and shopping for accessories with Katie.

Liz was not usually a girly girl, but she felt like one as she planned out the next two weeks. Emotionally drained, she fell asleep with pen in hand, making her to-do list.

CHAPTER SEVENTEEN

Early the next day, Ian was getting ready to go to his two-week follow up appointment. When someone knocked on his back door, his smile was automatic. He made himself walk to the door, but the child in him wanted to run and skip. That would be unnatural for a man his size, so he practiced restraint. He'd hoped Liz would pop over to tell him goodbye before she flew home to Georgia.

When he opened the door, his smile grew strained before it fell completely. Instead of the pretty red head he was so fond of, her ex-husband greeted him.

"Have you come to tell me off? Punch me in the face? Threaten my life?" He hoped no fists would fly toward his newly healed face.

"I came to tell you that I hope you can make her happy. She deserves every good thing in the world and none of the bad. I've always thought of her as mine, even after I wrecked our marriage. All these years, I've been holding onto her, hoping and praying she could love me again."

"Why are you telling me this?"

"Because, I don't think you deserve her either. I

think you're going to hurt her and if she lets me know about it, I'll be there to pick up the pieces and the next time I see you after that, I'll forget my raising."

"I've been warned. Fly safely and take care of *my* girl." Ian closed the door before Jason could respond.

He was certain Liz didn't know about her ex's visit. The thought of telling her just so she'd rip Jason a new one, as he'd heard her say, crossed his mind. But, that was beneath him. He should've handled it differently, but Jason had vexed him one time too many.

The truth was he had no idea where his relationship with Liz was going. He couldn't make promises to Jason or anyone else about how it would turn out. The premiere was a test to see how she handled herself with the Hollywood crowds. If it went according to plan, he'd wake up with her the morning after and convince her to go on holiday with him.

His agent wasn't thrilled when Ian told him his date was not in the business. Will had anticipated an up-and-coming actress whose name would generate buzz. Ian convinced him an unknown mystery woman would set chins to wagging. He found himself borrowing a lot of phrases from his Southern belle.

The following two weeks passed slowly for Ian as he anticipated Liz's return to Los Angeles. He couldn't believe how much he missed seeing her even though they spoke daily. She'd expressed how exceedingly nervous she was becoming as the time drew near.

Ian was anxious as well because he could see a change in his nose. The bump on the bridge of his nose, which had bothered him since it was broken at university and which no one complained about but Emma, was gone. He feared the press would notice.

He pushed the thoughts away. He'd need to conceal his anxiety to put Liz at ease.

He waited with Danny at the hanger for her to arrive. She was to be accompanied by Katie and her husband, Robert. Robert was an attorney and top aide to the Governor of Georgia, but he cleared his schedule to come keep Liz's wine glass full while she got ready for the premiere. Ian was very glad Jason wouldn't be along this trip.

When she walked down the stairway of the jet, she smiled at him and his feeble heart skipped a beat. She was radiant. She'd told him about a special conditioning treatment her hair stylist used and it shone like a copper penny. Between the hair and the sparkle in her eyes, she very nearly glowed.

Ian picked her up into a full body hug and she wrapped her arms around his neck.

"I missed you like crazy." She kissed his cheek.

"I didn't think it was possible, but you look even more beautiful than when I last saw you."

"I'm gonna have to get my waders out." She winked at him.

He put her feet on the ground and fought the urge to kiss her. He wanted their first kiss to be private, but it seemed they were never alone. He tore himself away from Liz to meet her sister and brother-in-law.

He could see some resemblance, but Katie was blonde and a few inches shorter than Liz, even in the world's tallest heels. Robert looked like a governor's aide: forties, expensive suit, dark hair distinguished with gray at the temples. Not a bad looking chap, if you were into barrister types.

Over dinner, Ian told Liz everything he thought she

needed to know about the premiere. She barely ate anything and he'd noticed she was slimmer when she got off the plane. He didn't dare comment on it since he'd made a big deal about it when he'd invited her. He wasn't going to disinvite her and truthfully, she looked fantastic.

Katie had helpful advice for Liz as well. She insisted they practice walking together and posing for photographs so they could see their best angles. Ian had never thought to practice beforehand, but he should have; he learned a great deal from the experience.

Liz put on the five-inch heels she'd be wearing and in the short skirt she wore, her legs never looked better. Robert was the photographer and Danny was the heckler. Ian couldn't remember having more fun with a group of friends. He requested Robert email him a few of the pictures.

Liz walked him out and before he told her goodnight, he told her what time he planned to pick her.

"I've a few last minute things to take care of in the morning, before my stylist comes over, so I won't see you until then."

She took a deep breath and let it out slowly. "I can do this."

"You'll be brilliant." He leaned in for a kiss and once again the back door opened.

This time she didn't jump away from him, but the kiss was shortened to a friendly peck.

"Family–can't live with 'em, can't drag 'em behind the car legally." She smiled.

Katie stood at the door. "Ian, be sure you get here in

time for us to take pictures before you leave."

"Feels like prom all over again," Liz said.

"This will be so much better, I promise." Ian kissed the back of her hand while looking into her eyes and enjoying the shudder which rolled over her. He released her and whistled as he strode home.

CHAPTER EIGHTEEN

Liz turned around to take a final look in the full-length mirror. She looked pretty good for a country girl. She had Taylor Swift hair, except for the color. Her eyes appeared bluer than ever. She attributed it to the combination of the copper tones of her eye make-up and the Caribbean blue dress.

"He's here," Katie trilled as she danced into the room. "He is so va-va-voom, I don't know how you stand it."

Liz put her hand on her stomach to settle the fireflies fluttering around. "I have to look past his exterior to the kind man behind those dreamy eyes. Sounds cheesy, I know. Why do I feel like a giddy teenager? And why are you acting like one?"

Katie performed a pirouette before she danced out the door. Liz let out a long slow breath and followed. She was telling herself, *it's just Ian, you know him, he's your friend*. That was until she set eyes on him. She might need help picking her jaw up off the floor.

Ian's suit fit him like a glove and she wanted to be the glove. She tried to push the memories from her mind of every time she'd seen his bare chest, but a visual bomb exploded in her brain. Every image sent her one step closer to jumping on him like a flea on a dog's butt. She blinked and made herself look into his eyes. Her Ian was there, in the blue-gray depths.

"Stop biting your lip, Lizabelle, you'll mess up your lipstick," Katie said.

"There aren't words to describe your beauty." Ian leaned in and kissed her cheek.

The words every woman wanted to hear spoken to her in a British accent by a handsome man who smelled like heaven.

She made the understatement of the century. "You clean up nice, too."

He proffered his arm. "Shall we?"

"Wait!" Katie said. "Robert, get the camera."

"Oh, blazes," Danny said. "Sorry, man. The Baker girls are the most photogenic women on the planet, so they never miss a chance for a photo shoot."

"That's good news actually." Ian winked.

After a few pictures, Liz tugged Ian to urge him out of Danny's house. "We'll never get away if we don't make a break for it."

"Let's crack on then."

Ian helped her into the limo and slid in beside her.

"I can't get over it, Liz. You're stunning."

"Thank you. You're more handsome than ever."

"Champagne?" He asked.

"I can't drink champagne."

It occurred to Liz that even though she and Ian spent two solid weeks together, they still didn't know enough about each other. She had a sinking feeling in her chest. This might be her last night with him. They hadn't made future plans and he was going to England to visit his family in two days.

"I think we also have beer."

"I'm good. I had a glass of wine or three while I was getting ready. But you go ahead."

"Are you all right, love?"

She wrung her hands. "I have a question. What are the chances that...I mean, how much...um, how much nudity are we talking about this episode? I need to be prepared. You know how I get and I'm sure you'd prefer I not watch the show with my hands over my face while I peek between my fingers."

Ian grinned and took her hand, interlacing their fingers. "Relax. If you must cover your eyes, go ahead, it won't bother me. There'll be lots of bare skin...on the screen. Look away if you must. I'll be right beside you, look at me instead."

He was being gracious. She wouldn't cover her face. It would embarrass him no matter what he said. Sooner than expected, the limo stopped and the door opened.

"Are you ready for the spotlight, love?"

"Naw. I'd rather do donuts in the parking lot in the back of this limo, motion sickness be damned." She took a deep breath and let it out slowly before she pasted on a smile. "Okay, I'm ready."

"Just hold onto me."

She held on like he was a lifeline. Bile rose in her throat when she first looked around at the crowd. There were people as far as she could see and many were shouting Ian's name. She looked up at him and he aimed his gorgeous smile at her. He patted her hand which gripped his bicep. Looking into his eyes, her smile became more natural and she relaxed to let her hand fall to his forearm. The turmoil inside died down and she took a stroll on the arm of her Hollywood hottie.

A few feet down the carpet, Ian moved his arm around her waist and guided her down the longest walk of her life. Katie's voice rang in her head: shoulders and elbows back, long neck, big smile, feet in third position, front knee bent. Pretty soon, Liz felt like she was eighteen again on the runway wearing a Clay Odom original; except for being in a shopping mall or at the Mart, she was on the red carpet, in L.A.

By the time Ian took her through the door of the venue, she was sure her face would fall off from all the smiling. "I need a drink."

"I knew you'd be brilliant." He hugged her close and kissed her cheek.

"Ian, Lizzie- hey, this is great, huh?" Bryan hugged Liz and shook Ian's hand.

"I wish I had your enthusiasm, Junior." Liz grinned.

"This is my date, Emily," Bryan said. "I met her with the dance you taught me, Lizzie."

Liz tried not to cringe. She'd always hated that nickname for some reason, but she liked Bryan so she didn't make a fuss over it. Ian handed her a glass of wine and she gave him a grateful smile.

"Are you an actress, too?" Emily asked.

Liz took a large swallow of wine. "No, I'm independently wealthy."

"What a kidder." Bryan punched Liz lightly in the arm.

"I hate to leave you, but we have to go back out for interviews," Ian said. "Will you be all right?"

"As long as *I* don't have to go back out there, I'll be

great. Go knock them off their feet...or whatever it is you handsome Hollywood types do." She squeezed his hand.

Liz chatted with Emily and a few other dates as they trickled in. She hovered near the open bar, though she didn't want to overdo it. When Ian returned, they went in to watch the premiere. She maintained a calm demeanor during the love scenes. Ian did look good naked. She knew they didn't paint those abs on and she was more than a little smug that the rest of the world didn't know about his tattoo.

They took a short limo ride to the after party at a swanky hotel. There was a banquet room with tables of food and drink, plus a DJ and dance floor. Liz was introduced to a lot of people she'd never remember. She got a lot of compliments on her dress, so she discreetly gave out Clay's business card. Why not? He'd taken care of her on short notice.

They ate and drank and danced. Ian was pretty tipsy and so was she. She'd never seen him drunk, only drugged. The effect seemed the same because he was more touchy feely, but she wasn't complaining.

When they were slow dancing, Ian leaned down to her ear. "Jason was right. Your legs do go on for miles when you wear heels."

Why did he have to mention Jason? His words sounded like a come-on instead of a compliment. She *should* be glad Ian noticed her legs. She *tried* to be glad.

When the song ended, they returned to their table. Liz took a seat in the chair where Ian's coat hung.

He put his hands on her shoulders. "I need to go check on something. Will you be okay here for a few moments?"

"Sure." She smiled trying to push Jason's words from Ian's mouth out of her head. She slid the nearly full wine glass away.

There was another woman at the table, the wife of one of the actors. She and Liz were close in age and they talked about fashion for a while before Liz pulled her phone from her clutch to check the time.

"Is something wrong?" The woman asked.

"Ian's been gone a while is all."

"He probably just went to your room to freshen up."

"Our room?"

"Yes, we always get rooms on premiere night. The party goes late."

"Oh." Liz ground her teeth with her perma-smile in place.

Why hadn't Ian mentioned it? Her heat dial was turning up and not in a sexy way. She didn't want to speculate. She'd just wait and ask him when he got back. She told herself to be flattered, but that dog wouldn't hunt.

Another half hour passed and Liz's shin ached because her constant foot tapping was out of control. She went to the bathroom and texted Ian. No response. She rolled her shoulders back and stretched her neck. Before she returned to the party, she checked the men's room. No Ian.

An hour later, she'd consumed a full pitcher of ice water while she tried to decide what to do. Other partygoers avoided her. Between her restless legs, crossed arms and hard smile, she couldn't blame them. On another trip to the bathroom, she detoured to the front desk.

"Hi, I'm Ian Clarke's date and he didn't tell me our room number. I don't suppose you could tell me."

"I'm sorry, madam, but we have a strict privacy policy."

"Could you call his room and tell him Liz is looking for him?"

The man looked like he was about to give her the heave ho, but he started typing on his computer. "I'm sorry, madam, there's no guest registered under that name."

Liz thought about possible aliases. "Try his character's name, Dr. Steven Duncan."

The man typed. "I'm sorry, madam."

"Thanks for trying, Javier." She read his name tag. "Madam."

She was about to walk away so she turned back and he leaned forward to speak in a low voice.

"I did see Mr. Clarke go up in the elevator. He also came back down, but Mr. Watson was waiting with a small group of people. Mr. Clarke got back on the elevator with them and I haven't seen them since. It was probably an hour ago."

Liz smiled, pulled a big bill out of her clutch and slid it across the counter to Javier. "Thanks again."

She went back to the party and waited another hour. She stood to go and saw Ian's coat. When she picked it up, she found his cell in the pocket.

On her way out, she ran into Bryan and Emily. They were stumbling and holding each other up.

"Have you seen Ian?"

"He's hammered. We smoked a big, fat..." Bryan's words turned into laughter and he nearly fell down.

Liz could barely understand him before the fit of

laughter.

"Do you know what room he's in?"

"Nope." He spit on the "p" sound and Liz wiped the spittle off of her cheek. "He wouldn't tell any of us, so you two could have privacy." Bryan waggled his brows suggestively.

Her throat burned and she swallowed hard. "Okay, good night, Bryan, Emily."

Liz hoped there would be a cab waiting outside the hotel. Luck was on her side even though she'd left her horseshoe belt buckle at home.

She walked into Danny's house and was relieved to find they were still out. After they watched the red carpet arrivals streamed online, they were going out to celebrate.

She showered and packed her suitcase. She'd been over and over what could have happened to Ian. She was worried about him, but she was angry and hurt that he'd abandon her. She was reasonably sure he hadn't done it on purpose, but it did nothing for the empty feeling in her chest.

She still had his coat and phone. She sent him another text message before she walked over to his house and left his coat on a chair near the back door. She didn't know what else to do, so she starting making up stories to tell her family.

She kept picturing Bryan's face and disappointment settled on her slumped shoulders. The heaviness in her limbs and the dread in her heart wouldn't go away. That wasn't the Ian she knew. But then, maybe she really didn't know him very well.

She had to get out of town. She couldn't face him or her family. It was only a few hours to sunrise, so she ordered an Uber and left a note for Danny. She'd felt like a teenager for the last two weeks, so she decided to do the immature thing and run away.

CHAPTER NINETEEN

Loud knocking forced Ian to open his eyes. He closed them against the light filtering through the sheer hotel curtains.

"Housekeeping."

He moaned and turned over in the bed. His stomach roiled.

"Liz," he croaked, his throat dry and scratchy.

The knocking resounded again. He made his way to the door and opened it to a Hispanic woman.

"Housekeeping."

"We have late checkout."

"Yes, late checkout is three o'clock. It's that time now." She pointed to her watch.

Ian took a step back and scratched his head. How had he lost most of a day?

"Liz." He turned to the bathroom then back to the housekeeper. "Could you give us ten minutes to pack up please?"

She nodded. "I'll be back soon."

Ian checked the bathroom, but there was no sign of Liz anywhere in the suite. She must have gone home without him, but why wouldn't she wake him? He thought back to the previous evening as he threw things into a suitcase. He took the wine and glasses he'd brought, but left the flowers. There were too many to carry.

The last time he remembered seeing Liz was when he came up to make sure everything was set for the romantic evening he'd planned. When he ran into Bryan and company on the way back to the party, they'd talked him into going to Bryan's room for tequila shots. While there, someone produced a marijuana cigarette which passed to him a few times. The rest was a blur.

Oh no! If the last time he remembered seeing Liz was then, when he told her he'd be gone a few minutes, she must have given up and gone home. He looked for his phone to call her, but he couldn't find his jacket.

There was another knock at the door. He took one final look around and grabbed his luggage. He would have to make it up to Liz...if she was still speaking to him.

He got home and walked straight out the back door where he discovered his jacket. He took his phone from the pocket and checked it; two texts from Liz. The first one read: *Where are you???* The second: *Jason was right. Fairy tales end.*

He was in big trouble. He didn't know what Jason had to do with anything, but the last message didn't give him hope.

He knocked on Danny's back door and it swung open.

"What did you do to my sister?"

Ian took a step back. "I...nothing...I don't know. Is

she here? May I see her?"

"Come in. I just got back from the airport, where I dropped Katie and Robert. They think you two have gone to Vegas to elope."

"Why would they think that?"

Danny handed him a note written in Liz's precise hand.

D,

Premiere was something else. Taking a little trip. Will text you later.

Love you,

L

"Where did she go?" Ian asked.

"That's what I'd like to know. She was gone when we got in about three thirty this morning."

Ian explained what he remembered and showed Danny the messages from Liz. "I don't know what this last one means."

"I do." He passed the phone back. "What you're telling me is that you got wasted and passed out in a hotel room and left my sister at a premiere party by herself."

"Yes." Ian dropped his head into his hands. "I know she may never speak to me again, but I want to be sure she's all right. I should've taken better care of her."

"Have you talked to Bryan? Did anyone else who smoked that weed have a similar reaction?"

Ian called Bryan while Danny waited with his arms crossed over his chest.

"Bryan doesn't remember anything, but his date didn't smoke it and she remembered seeing Liz. Emily said Bryan told her about the hotel room and made suggestive comments."

"Did Liz know about the room?"

"I wanted to surprise her. I got flowers and wine...never mind...you don't want to hear how I intended to romance your sister and make her fall in love with me."

Danny stared at the floor for a moment. "Ian, you don't realize how bad an idea the hotel room was. Not telling her beforehand was especially bad. Liz had something happen to her."

Ian's whole body tensed and a fresh wave of nausea hit him. "Please don't tell me—"

"Almost," Danny cut him off. "She fought him off and got away before the worst thing happened. He was a friend. Someone she'd been hanging out with, but not dating. They got really wasted at a bar and neither of them could drive, so he suggested a hotel. She trusted him. She was asleep in one of the beds by herself and woke up with him on top of her."

"Bloody wanker."

"Like I said, she got away, but I'm sure the memory probably hit her hard last night when she found out you'd gotten a room and didn't mention it to her."

Ian ran his hand through his hair. "I had no idea. I hope you know I'd never harm Liz. I would never force myself on her, or anyone else for that matter."

"I believe you. I think you really care about my sister."

"I do." Ian nodded as he spoke.

"And I think she cares about you, but I'm sure she's pretty hurt right now. The fairy tale thing — that's what Jason told her when he tried to talk her out of going to the premiere."

"What can I do?"

"I have an idea where she might be. I'll find her and talk to her and let you know from there."

"I leave for England tomorrow. I could postpone."

"Don't change your plans. Lizabelle is going to need a cool down period. She can be a hot-head when she wants to be. It's the red hair."

Ian smiled at the memory Danny's words recalled; a cold shower on a hot day. The smile faded as his heart squeezed. He may have lost her and Jason was right again. Ian didn't deserve Liz.

***

Liz dug her toes into the warm sand as she sat in the late afternoon June sun and watched the blue-gray water of the Atlantic churn and chop. The color reminded her of Ian's eyes.

It had been two days since she boarded the commercial plane to Jacksonville, Florida from LAX. She had a condo in the sleepy Georgia coastal town of Quiet Cove, slightly north of the state line. She might as well enjoy it while she hid from everyone who loved her. She'd been getting calls and text messages from her family which she mostly ignored, but nothing from Ian. She only responded to her family to let them know she was *not* married.

She was far from it and at the rate she was going, it wasn't ever going to happen again. She sighed, resigned to the spinster life. She had nieces and nephews to spoil. Maybe one of them would visit her in the nursing home when she was old and alone.

"Nice view."

She looked up to see Danny strolling toward her.

"Yeah, this property is for sale. I was thinking about buying and building a house here."

"I saw a nice place for sale back that way." He gave a quick nod back over his shoulder. "Maybe I'll buy it and we can be neighbors."

"Deal. How'd you find me?"

"High-tech spy stuff."

She laughed. "You refuse to use the GPS in your truck, but you track me with high-tech spy equipment?"

One corner of his mouth quirked up. "I know you, Lizabelle. I know how you think. What happened?"

Liz glanced up at him. "You already know what happened."

"I want to hear you tell it." He sat next to her on the sand.

They talked it out and in the end she admitted she felt like a fool.

"Were you afraid of Ian? That he might...you know...like last time?"

She shook her head. "No. In fact, I wanted him pretty bad, but...he's never even kissed me. Not for real. I'm not sure he likes me that way."

Danny raised an eyebrow. "What're you gonna do now?"

"Lick my wounds here for a few days, maybe buy this oceanfront property. Then, I'll put on my big girl panties and go back home."

"You should talk to Ian."

She punched the sand. "Don't want to. Plus, he should be in England by now."

"There's a new invention...a thing called a telephone–they even have them in foreign countries. You should at least let him apologize."

Liz picked up a fist full of sand and watched it fall

through her fingers as she opened her hand. "I need time."

"If you really care about him, don't take too long. He might slip through your fingers."

It only took a few days for Liz to get the paperwork taken care of for her new property. Then, she went home.

The kids were out of school and wanted Aunt Lizabelle to play with them at Southland. She certainly needed the distraction the kids could provide. What she didn't need was the barrage of questions. They wanted to know every detail of her Cinderella at the ball story.

Jason was on her mind a lot since he'd predicted her downfall. The good thing was he didn't know about it. No one but Danny knew the truth. She'd come up with an alternative reality to explain the evening. Sticking with the Cinderella theme, she told them she turned into a pumpkin. The party was going late, she was tired, so she left Ian to enjoy himself.

It was tricky explaining why she'd left L.A. in the middle of the night, but since she took an early flight, she hedged her way through the falsehood. Katie and Robert had partied hard that night since they were out of the political limelight of Georgia, so they didn't question her departure time.

They did question her decision to go to her condo because they thought she'd spend as much time with Ian as possible before he left for England. She'd said they'd decided it would be harder to separate if they spent more time together. As lies went, it was weak. She hated being dishonest with her family, but if by some miracle Ian called and she accepted his apology, she didn't want her family to hate him.

Part of her wanted him to call and part of her didn't. There was no future with Ian. She needed to move on. Plus, he'd had plenty of time to make up his own version of what happened to him that night. To lessen the chances of having to talk to him, she left her cell phone in her room at Southland while she played in the heat of July surrounded by the only children she would ever have a hand in raising.

CHAPTER TWENTY

Ian paced the floor of his London flat. He'd spent the first week at his parents' home. The second week, he stayed at his flat and spent his evenings with his siblings and their families.

It was an important day. Ringing Liz was top priority. Danny told him to try calling her in two weeks, but it was still early in America and he didn't want to wake her.

He'd been driving his family mad talking about Liz and how he missed her. They didn't understand why he had to wait to call her. It was difficult for him to abide, but Danny knew her best and he didn't want to cock it up again.

At the appropriate time, he called. He swallowed and wiped his palms in anticipation. The call went to voicemail. He hadn't expected that, he should've, but in the scenario in his mind, she always answered his calls. He didn't intend to leave an apology message. He hadn't worked one out. He disconnected before the beep and tried to decide his next move. Perhaps she'd see the missed call and ring him back.

After speaking with Danny, Ian decided to call each

day and leave a message until she answered. A week later, she hadn't answered his voice or text messages. Danny wasn't getting much response from her either.

"You should go to her. A face-to-face apology will work. How can she say no to this face?" His mum cupped his cheek.

"I don't know, Mum. She must've decided against me."

"Impossible, love. I've seen the photographs. The way you two look at each other, well, there's something there. She was hurt by your actions because she cares for you. Go, bring her to meet us."

Ian ran the idea by Danny and since he was in favor of it, he landed in Atlanta on a Friday evening in July. He checked into a hotel, not wanting to impose on Liz, especially if she had not forgiven him. It was not yet nine o'clock so Ian drove his rental car to her house and parked on the street when he saw the lights were on. He took a deep breath and walked to the front door.

A man answered. Ian recognized him from photographs as one of her brothers.

"Ian Clarke." The man extended his hand. "How the heck are you?"

"Very well, thanks." Ian shook his hand. "You are John, correct?"

"Right on, but everybody calls me Johnny. Come on in."

Ian was relieved he guessed the right brother. The front door opened into the open living area and there was a small boy asleep on the sofa. Ian couldn't recall the name of Johnny's son.

"Liz didn't tell us you were coming. She thinks

you're across the pond."

"Ah, yes, I'd rather thought to surprise your sister. Is she not home?"

"Nah, she's playing at the bar tonight. I'm heading over there to pick her up, if my ex ever shows up to get my boy." Johnny gestured to the sleeping child.

A horn honked outside and Johnny peeked out the window. "There she is, the little so and so." He picked his son up and carried him outside. When he returned, he said, "You can ride with me if you want."

"I'm not sure surprising Liz there is a good idea."

"Sure it is. She'll be thrilled to see you. She's been acting weird. Must be 'cause she's been missin' ya."

Ian was hesitant. Approaching Liz in a public place could go well, or it could go badly.

"If you're worried about being seen by fans and what not, I can get you into the sound booth. You can see everything from there, but not be seen, if that makes sense."

"It does. Lead on, mate."

Johnny led Ian in a back door and into the booth where he was introduced to the sound technician, a heavy man called Tiny. From his vantage point, he had a great view of Liz onstage. She wore a denim dress and red boots to match her red guitar.

She stood near the front of the stage a few feet away from Jason. The rest of the band was a little behind them.

"There's usually another girl who sings lead vocals, but she's not here tonight, so Lizabelle has to do it." Johnny handed him a bottle of beer.

"She's quite good."

"She's a rock star, but don't tell her I said so. I

wouldn't want her to get the big head, especially since she's been to a Hollywood premiere," Johnny said with a smirk.

By the time the house lights came on, they'd each had a few bottles of beer. Ian couldn't keep his eyes off Liz. Even though the glamour factor was dialed down, she was captivating. He feared his heart was no longer his own.

"Who is that man?" Ian asked Johnny. There was a tall, blond man hugging Liz a bit too closely.

"Well, I'll be darned. That's Chris Ross."

"Bollocks." Ian watched in agony as Liz and Chris exchanged phones, presumably to get each other's number. He might be too late.

Chris gave her another hug before he left and Liz watched him walk away. Then she turned in the direction of the booth.

"Johnny," she said as Johnny stepped out of the booth. Ian was behind two-way glass and she hadn't seen him. "Come grab my guitar, I forgot to tell Jason something."

"Here he comes." Johnny pointed. "What did Chris want?"

"A date. He just moved back to town. I'm shocked because I thought I was the reason he left."

"Hockey," Johnny said.

"Here, Lizabelle." Jason tried to hand her a wad of cash.

She pushed his hand away. "Roxanne could use it. Make sure she gets it for me."

Jason kissed her cheek. "You're a good woman. I saw Chris last week and he asked about you. I told him where you'd be tonight."

Liz smiled and squeezed Jason's arm. "Thanks, I think."

"I brought you a surprise, Lizabelle," Johnny said.

Ian stepped down out of the booth with more than a little trepidation.

"Dangit, they're coming out of the woodwork." Jason spun on his heel and strode away.

Ian fixed his eyes on the woman he'd traveled so far to see. His heart lurched, but he stood perfectly still to gauge her reaction. He was poised to run, but whether it was toward her or away, he didn't yet know.

***

The guitar case slipped from Liz's grasp and landed with a dull thud. She was certain she was more jostled than her guitar. It was protected by a hard exterior and a cushioned lining, unlike her heart which dropped to her stomach at the sight of Ian.

She swallowed hard, her throat suddenly thick. "This is a surprise, brother, straight from the Motherland."

"I hope it's not an unwelcome surprise. I tried to ring you, but apparently your phone isn't working."

Liz's face warmed. She'd gotten his messages and she wanted to call him back, but she didn't know what to say. She was ashamed for having run away and not being brave enough to take his calls.

"You need to change you service provider, Lizabelle. In her defense, she's been at Southland for the past two weeks with kids coming out of her ears. Her cell reception there is spotty at best."

"That explains it then." Ian revealed a small smile.

The twinkle in his eyes let her know he was letting her off the hook. She didn't want to get into it in front of her brother anyway. Johnny was more protective than Jason and Danny combined.

Ian opened his arms in an inviting gesture and Liz stepped into his embrace. She inhaled his scent and enjoyed the feel of his big arms around her. He was familiar and foreign at the same time.

Johnny cleared his throat. "Get a room. Speaking of, Liz, Ian got a hotel room. I told him we weren't having it since you have an available guest room, but he insisted on talking to you first."

Liz tensed at the mention of a hotel room, but relaxed when she realized what her brother was saying. Ian rubbed her back and his eyes held sympathy.

Liz had to swallow again before she could speak. "You're very welcome to stay at my house. Johnny is staying the night as well."

"I hope to be in town beyond one night and I don't want to take advantage of your hospitality. Don't let your brother push you to make a decision just yet. I'll stay in the room I've let and we can talk tomorrow."

"If you prefer to stay in your own space, I understand—"

He cut her off. "Don't misunderstand, Liz. I *want* to stay with you. I traveled more than four thousand miles to see you, but I'm not going to force myself on you. I would *never* do that." He used a finger to push her hair back over her ear.

As long as he was sober, she trusted him. The day of his surgery had replayed in her mind a thousand times. What she had brushed off as innocent flirtation, she now viewed in a more sinister light. He'd never fully understand if she didn't tell him, although she was sure bringing it up would cause embarrassment for them both.

"Um...where's your ride?" She asked.

"He rode with me, but his rental is in front of your house." Johnny picked up the guitar case.

"Let's go," she said. "We can talk in the truck."

"Liz."

She turned to see Roxanne approaching with tears in her eyes. She hugged her hard. "Thank you. You don't know what this means to me."

"You just take care of your sweet boy. I'm glad to help." Liz winked at Roxanne and squeezed her arm when she pulled back.

Roxanne was a single mom with no medical insurance and her son had a broken arm. She attended community college by day and waited tables at the bar at night. Liz had already arranged to pay her rent for a year and had her parents agree to say they'd done it. She was getting better at lying because her dad was teaching her to be generous and sneaky about it. She loved having the means to help others. Philanthropy was her calling.

Liz slid into the center of the bench seat in Johnny's old truck and Ian got in beside her. It was hard to look at him, not knowing where they stood exactly. She'd never been on even footing with Ian and she didn't think she ever would be. He was on his way to superstardom and she preferred a simpler kind of life.

CHAPTER TWENTY-ONE

Ian knocked on Liz's door the next morning. She'd told him to park and come in the back. Johnny had already left for Southland, so they sat at the kitchen bar and talked over coffee.

"I promise to never do drugs again." He made circles on the back of her hand.

"I got a hold of some amped weed once. I thought I'd lost my mind. Drugs and I don't mix very well," Liz said as she picked up her coffee cup.

"Jason did mention something about that," Ian said.

At the look Liz gave him, he asked, "What? I've said something that displeases you."

"The night of the premiere, you repeated something Jason said and it bothered me. I mean, I'm used to Jason saying sleazy things to me, but not you."

"What did I say?"

She reminded him.

"Please accept my apology. I would never intentionally—"

"There's something else," she interrupted. She told him about what he'd said and done after his surgery.

"It's no wonder you don't trust me. You must think

157

I'm a real wanker."

"It's not that. I just felt the need to point out that mind altering chemicals can make people behave differently than they normally would. I don't trust anyone who overdoes it. I'm sorry, I know I'm coming across as judgmental and self-righteous, but I've been there."

"Don't apologize, love." He squeezed her hand. "I'd prefer you be honest and tell me what troubles you. I regret the mistakes I made the night of the premiere. I should've looked after you better."

"It was your big night, Ian. You deserved to have fun without having to babysit me. I should've been more prepared."

"I invited you. It was my duty to make you comfortable and ensure you had a good time. I should've told you about the room. Regrettably, I was an epic failure that night."

"Don't say that. We had fun for a while." She smiled.

"You are very gracious—" He was interrupted by Liz's phone. "We need to chuck our phones."

She laughed as she answered. "Hey, Mama, can I call you back?" Her eyebrows drew together. "What? Slow down, I can't understand you."

Her face paled and she stood and paced. "Are you at the hospital now?"

Fear crept into Ian's heart. He tried to say a prayer, but wasn't sure what to ask for.

"I'll call Johnny and Aunt Nancy. Take some deep breaths and try to calm down, it won't help Big Daddy if you have a heart attack, too. Call me if they life-flight him over here. I'll call the troops. I love you,

Mama."

"Your father?" He asked and she nodded as tears filled her eyes. "What can I do?"

"I need to make some calls."

Ian got her a glass of water and a box of tissues and stood behind her rubbing her shoulders while she called everyone. Her mom called back to report they were flying her father to Atlanta for surgery.

When she spoke to Danny, her voice cracked for the first time. Ian wished he could absorb her pain.

"Ian is here with me." After a beat, she passed the phone to him.

"Danny, I'm sorry about your father."

"Listen, stay with her. She'll try to handle everything on her own. I'm flying out as soon as I call my pilot and pack a bag."

"I'm not going anywhere. Safe travels, mate."

Liz spent the next half hour making and taking phone calls. Ian answered the house phone when she was on her cell.

Jason came in the back door in a rush. He went directly to Liz and pulled her off her stool into a tight embrace. Ian's muscles bunched and he turned away, pushing down the envy. It was not the time to mark his territory. She let go of Jason to answer her phone.

"Anything new to report?" Jason asked Ian.

"Not to my knowledge."

"Did Mama D hear the knocks?"

Ian furrowed his brow. "Pardon?"

Liz hung up. "Johnny and Mama are about half-way here. They want me to go on up to the hospital in case I can see Big Daddy before they take him back for surgery."

"I'll drive," Jason said.

Liz sat in the center and Ian put his arm around her. She leaned into him.

"Everything will be all right, love." Ian hoped it was true.

"He's right, Lizabelle. Big Dan is tough as nails. If anyone can survive this, he can."

"Tell me about him, Liz." He took one of her hands in his and twined their fingers.

"His friends call him Big Dan. Maddie started calling him Big Daddy to differentiate from our biological father when he adopted us and it stuck..."

Ian was glad to have her talking. It was worse when she was quiet because it meant she was thinking and possibly imagining the worst.

The ride to the hospital wasn't very long and once there, they met Liz's brother-in-law, Mark. He was a surgeon, though not a cardiologist.

"You're just in time to see him before they prep him for surgery, Lizabelle." Mark put his arm around her and led her through a set of double doors.

Ian waited with Jason. To borrow an expression from Liz, it was awkward as asphalt.

"You said something about knocks?" Ian asked to make conversation.

"Yeah, if Liz hasn't told you, I'm not going to. It's a family thing. You probably wouldn't understand anyway. Lord knows I didn't at first. I thought her mama was crazy as all get out."

"Is she? Crazy?"

"No, she's a good woman." Jason dropped his shoulders and lifted his chest.

"Jase."

They both turned to see a younger version of Liz walking toward them. Ian blinked hard.

"Maddie." Jason hugged her tight. "I'm so sorry, sweetheart. Mark took Liz back."

"Good, I don't want to see him. She can handle it, but I'll lose it."

"Maddie, this is Ian. Maddie is Mark's better half."

Ian examined Liz's youngest sister. He'd seen pictures, but in person her mannerisms reminded him of Liz and the resemblance was remarkable. He couldn't help but smile.

She wiped her face with her hands. "I'd shake your hand, but I don't want to get snot all over you."

"Understood. I'm sorry about your father." He wished he had something more comforting to say.

Jason pulled a handkerchief from his back pocket and gave it to her. He kept his arm around her while she sniveled. Mark came out and went to console his wife. Ian looked toward the double doors, but Liz didn't appear.

***

Liz's chest hitched as she drew a shaky breath when she saw Big Daddy pale and lifeless with oxygen and IV drugs doing their best to keep him alive.

"Hey, you mean thang." Her voice cracked, but she forced a smile. "If you wanted some attention, you didn't have to go to all this trouble."

He tried to laugh. She took his hand being careful of the needle in his wrist. "You're gonna be okay. You have to at least make it to see your Baker's dozen grandkids be born."

"Lizabelle." His voice was a whisper and she leaned closer. "They're gonna fix me up..." He stopped to catch his breath. "I'll be out of here in no time. You know you can't keep a good man down."

Liz laughed and brushed his hair back. "I know, Daddy, and you're the best man. We'll be right here when you wake up from surgery. Danny will probably be here by then."

"You tell him..." He took a big breath. "You tell all of my kids that Big Daddy loves 'em...tell your mama too —"

"You can tell them your damn self, when you wake up."

"Where'd you learn to talk like that?"

"From you, who else?"

"Miss Baker, we need to take him back now," a nurse said.

Liz leaned down and kissed her daddy's clammy cheek. "I love you, Daddy."

"I love you too, my girl."

When he was out of sight, the dam broke. The barriers she carefully constructed to hold the sorrow back crumbled and she struggled to breathe. She couldn't focus, didn't know where to turn.

"Miss, may I show you to the restroom?"

She nodded and blindly followed the stranger. She had no idea how long she cried in the ladies' room, but it was long enough to make her face irreparable. Her eyes were swollen and red, her cheeks were splotchy, and her neck and chest looked sunburned.

There was a knock on the door. Whoever waited was probably about to explode since she'd been in there so long. She opened the door and barely registered Ian standing in front of her before he crushed her against his chest. She'd been mistaken in believing she was all cried out, because the floodgates opened again.

"Shh, my love, everything will turn out right. You'll see." He smoothed her hair and rubbed her back.

So much for looking pretty for the always-gorgeous Ian Clarke. If he could still stand to look at her after seeing her ugly cry, he was a keeper.

"I'm glad you're here with me," she said when the worst was over.

"I wouldn't want to be anywhere else. I don't know what to do, so please tell me if I can help you or any of your family."

"What you're doing right now is really, really perfect."

She felt him chuckle and press his lips on the top of her head. "I'm at your service. By the way, some of your family has arrived."

"I'm sorry." She pulled away and reached for the tissue. "I should've been there to introduce you."

"Already done. Between Katie, Robert, and Jason, I've been thoroughly introduced. Maddie said your mum and Johnny should be here very soon."

"I suppose I better suck it up and go out there." She rubbed her eyes.

"Take your time. We'll go when you're ready." His tone was gentle. "Will you tell me about the knocks?"

"Well..." Liz cleared her throat. It was hard to explain, but any man with a horseshoe tattooed on his torso might be a little superstitious, so he might accept it. "My mom gets premonitions before someone close to her passes away. She calls it the death knocks. It's three knocks and the death occurs in three days."

"Has she heard them recently?"

Liz let out a sigh. If he wasn't making fun of her, it was a good sign. "Let's go find out."

Extended family and friends arrived and the Operating Room waiting area got crowded. Liz got hugs from all of her brothers, sisters, nieces, nephews, in-laws and out-laws and made sure they'd been introduced to Ian. To everyone's relief, Mama hadn't heard the knocks.

Jason picked Danny up from the airport and when they got to the hospital, Liz lost it again. Danny gave her a long hug and she told him about her conversation with their dad.

The cardiologist came out to say the surgery was successful and the patient was doing well. They planned to keep him in the cardiac unit overnight and move him to a private room the next day.

"I can let two of you back to see him in recovery," the doctor said.

Everyone looked around at each other, but Liz spoke up. "Danny and Mama should go."

Murmurs of agreement filled the air and Liz smiled as Danny took her mom's hand. When their parents married, he'd been the most resistant. Thankfully, her mama was understanding and loved Danny despite his standoffish attitude.

Katie invited everyone to her house for dinner. "Rosa has been cooking all day." Rosa was their live-in housekeeper.

Anyone who didn't already live in Atlanta was invited to stay there, too. Katie and Robert's home was a Colonial mansion in Buckhead complete with maid's quarters, pool house, and guest house.

After dinner, Liz was exhausted. Danny had picked

up her truck when he'd gotten to town, so Liz and Ian told everyone goodnight and returned to her place.

Once inside, the phone rang and Liz groaned in frustration.

"May I?" Ian asked before answering.

He held the phone to her with a smirk on his face. "It's Chris Ross."

As soon as Liz had the phone in her hand, the doorbell rang. Ian went to answer it.

"Hey Chris, you aren't at my front door are you?"

"No, why?"

"Never mind, what's up?"

Ian opened the door and Johnny's ex-wife, Tiffany, stood on the porch holding her sleeping son, Nick.

"Oh my God! You're Ian Clarke. Oh my God. I love you." Tiffany's eyes were as big as saucers.

Liz was listening to both Tiffany and Chris and trying to decide who to respond to.

"Chris, can you hold on for a minute?" She held the phone down. "Tif, what's up?"

"Isn't Johnny here? Nick wanted to stay with him so he can see Big Daddy tomorrow."

"Danny is staying here and Johnny is at Katie's."

Tiffany huffed and scrunched up her face.

"Just leave him with me," Liz said.

"I'll take him," Ian said.

"Thank you," Liz told him.

Tiffany got the thrill of her life as she handed her four-year-old over to Ian. Liz didn't like the hungry look in her eyes so she stepped between them and took Nick's bag.

"Good night, Tif." Liz closed the door on the starry eyed woman.

"Gosh, I hope I didn't drool over you like that. Put him in my bed. Oh, and make sure he's wearing a pull up. He still leaks at night sometimes."

She put the phone back to her ear. "Sorry about that, Chris." While Ian put Nick to bed, Liz took a few moments to thank Chris for calling and promised to keep him posted on her dad's health.

"Nick is all settled. Would you like a drink?" Ian asked after Liz disconnected from her call with Chris.

"I'd love one." She sank onto the couch.

They each had a beer and when she told him good night, she touched his arm. "Ian, thank you for being there for me today."

He closed the distance between them and slowly lowered his mouth to hers. It was the sweetest kiss she'd ever had. Heat spread from her lips to her toes. It was a good thing Nick was in her bed and Danny would be home soon or she'd be tempted to give into some much needed comfort and distraction.

"Goodnight." He walked into his room and closed the door.

She put her fingers to her lips wondering if it had been real. The memory of his lips would haunt her dreams.

CHAPTER TWENTY-TWO

Ian stood in Liz's bedroom doorway the next morning and smiled at the sight before him. Liz was on the edge of the bed, curled up with a small blanket covering her. Nick was sprawled sideways across the bed with his head in Liz's back.

The little boy opened his eyes and stretched. Ian put a finger over his lips hoping Nick would be quiet and not wake Liz.

"Do you want to help me with breakfast?" Ian whispered.

Nick nodded and rolled off the bed. Ian closed the bedroom door.

"Hi, Nick, I'm Ian." He extended his hand and the little boy shook it.

"I saw your picture with Aunt Lizabelle on the computer. She looked really pretty."

"Yes, she did. I was very lucky to have her agree to be my date."

"Are you her boyfriend?"

"Why don't you ask her that question later, when we serve her breakfast in bed?" Ian assisted as Nick climbed onto the high stool at the eat-in bar in the kitchen.

"Okay." Nick requested chocolate milk and while Ian made it, the boy started with the Q& A game.

"Do you like video games?" Was the first of many questions Nick had for Ian while he made pancakes and bacon.

"Do you want to put the blueberries in?" Ian asked.

Nick set his glass of chocolate milk down and leaned over the counter to pour the berries into the batter. Ian smiled at the milk mustache he sported.

Ian prepared a tray for Liz while Nick ate his pancakes. Before they took it in, Ian put his finger on his chin. "I wish we had a flower to put on the tray."

Nick's eyes grew wider. "I know, I know, come with me."

He followed Nick out onto the back deck and down the stairs to the flower bed. There was a small bed of orange daylilies. Ian smiled knowing lilies was one of her favorites. He let Nick pick one and they put it in a small vase of water.

"You get the door, I'll carry the platter."

Nick opened the door, ran into the room and jumped on the bed. "Wake up, Aunt Lizabelle. Me and Ian made pancakes."

Liz pushed herself up and slid over so Ian could sit on the edge of the bed. She looked great first thing in the morning. Of course, her hair had been dry when she went to sleep. He smiled at the memory.

"You've been busy." She inhaled deeply. "It smells delicious."

"It tastes yummy. I already ate mine," Nick said.

"This is a very pretty flower." She touched the petals.

"I picked it," Nick said. "But it was Ian's idea."

"Are you forgetting something, Nick?" She asked.

His brow furrowed as his eyes rolled up and to the left.

"We don't call grown-ups by their first names, do we?"

He bit his lip. "I forgot, sorry, Mr. Ian."

"It's quite all right, Nick."

"Hey, Aunt Lizabelle, is Mr. Ian your boyfriend?"

A slow smile spread across her face. "Did you ask him?"

"He said to ask you," Nick said. "What's the big deal? He's a boy and he's your friend."

"Well, when you put it like that, I guess the answer is yes. If he keeps making me breakfast in bed, I might keep him."

The cross eyed look she gave Ian did nothing to squelch his joy or attraction to her. He was glad to hear he was her boyfriend, as strange as it sounded for two people over thirty-five.

They chatted while Liz ate and then Nick followed Ian back to the kitchen to clean up while Liz got ready. Danny joined them and they made plans to go back to the hospital.

While Liz was getting Nick dressed, Johnny came in. "I've got a news flash for you people."

"We've got one for you, too," Danny said. "Your offspring is here."

"I wondered. Tif said she'd bring him to me and when she didn't, I assumed she changed her mind."

"She thought you were still here," Danny said.

"Oops," Johnny said. "Hey, did she happen to see you, Ian?"

"Yes, I took Nick from her because Liz was on the phone."

"That might explain why there are reporters at the hospital," he said. "She got a big mouth, probably Tweeted and Facebooked and all that jazz."

"Why didn't you lead off with that news?" Danny asked.

"Because, I was rudely interrupted by my big brother." Johnny put his hands on his hips.

"Daddy." Nick ran into the kitchen, followed by Liz.

"Sister, the secret's out. They know Ian's in town. What do y'all want to do?" Danny asked.

Ian didn't want to be forced out of Liz's life by the press. He hoped she'd want him to stay.

She sighed. "I reckon I better put on some more makeup."

Ian sent up a silent "thank you" to the heavens and put his arm around her. She returned his embrace.

"Danny, this is your area of expertise. You tell us how to handle it," she said.

"I'll call hospital security to see if there's private parking and access they'll let us use. I'll also give my friends at Atlanta PD a heads up, in case they find out where you live."

They got busy and were ready to go half an hour later. Johnny took Nick in his truck and Danny drove Liz and Ian in her SUV. They had permission to park in an employee parking area with security and private entry.

They joined their family members in the waiting room of the Cardiac Unit. Some of the other grown children had been in to see their father already. The doctor still planned to move him later in the day.

Danny briefed the family on some ways to deal with the media. Ian was also able to contribute, but he mostly advised Liz, since she was the one most likely to get caught in the frenzy.

"Try to move past them if you can. Don't answer their questions. Don't run and don't cover your face. They'll think you have something to hide and that'll make it worse.

"Also, try to keep a pleasant expression on your face, because if you make a mean face, that'll be the one they post and print," Ian said.

"Liz, I've seen them form a wall with their bodies so you can't get through," Danny said. "If they catch you alone and one of us isn't there to muscle past them, you have two choices. You can turn around, go another direction, but the problem with that is you can still get yourself boxed in if they follow you. The other choice is to pick the weakest link and make them move. You know how to do that."

"A side kick to the kneecap? Or a front kick to the side of the knee?" she asked.

"A mule kick to the head would do it," Johnny said.

***

Liz ran a shaky hand through her hair. She nodded at each piece of advice, but her mind was numb. Her skin began to itch in unconnected places. She wanted to focus on her family and Big Daddy in particular. She didn't blame Ian and so far, there was talk of the press, but she hadn't actually seen them. But, she had enough to deal with. Worrying about one more thing threatened to push her over the edge.

Late in the afternoon, the nurse came to tell them

there were no private rooms available so they were keeping Big Daddy in the unit another night.

Katie invited everyone back to her house. "Guess what comes on tonight?"

Oh no, Liz thought as someone said, "Trauma."

"It comes on at ten," Katie said. "So we'll have time to eat and play before we put the kids to bed." Everyone was excited.

Liz turned to Ian. "If it makes you uncomfortable, we can leave before the show comes on."

"Does it make you uncomfortable?" He asked, taking her hands in his.

"You know how I am, but it would make their day to watch it with you." She gestured toward her family.

"Perhaps they can give me feedback like you did. It was very helpful." He twisted a section of her hair around his finger.

"Be careful what you wish for. With this crew, you're liable to get tips on everything from kissing to...well, let's just say it might get personal."

"Thanks for the heads-up." He kissed her cheek and took her hand in his.

They all piled into the elevator. Liz, Ian and Danny moved to the back since they were getting off after the others. The kids were already at Katie's because their youngest brother, Paul, and his wife had taken them so they could swim and play and not drive the other waiting family members insane.

When the elevator door opened, cameras flashed as Ian's name was called. Several things happened at once.

Robert and Katie were near the front so they stepped off first. Robert covered his face and said, "No pictures, please." Katie gave them her best pageant pose and said, "This is my best side."

Johnny and Jason moved in front of the photographers, there were only three. Maddie took one of Mama D's arms and Mark took the other as they exited the elevator.

Ian pulled Liz close to his side and she put her face in his chest and cackled. Danny pressed the close door button. The photographers couldn't get past Johnny and Jason.

"That went well," Danny said as he used the security badge to access the secure level.

"I love your family." Ian kissed her head. "That was quite fun."

"I think it's safe to say they think a lot of you, too," she said.

"We protect our own," Danny said.

***

After dinner, the group hung around the pool while the kids swam. Country music was playing low in the background.

Ian was seated behind Liz on a chaise lounge. He leaned up and put his lips next to her ear. "I'd like a dance. Would you do me the honor?"

"Here? Now?" She turned her head so their faces were very close.

"Why not?"

"I can't think of a reason." She stood as he gave her little boost.

He moved them away from the adults and closer to the music. He held her close and she relished the feel of him as everything else faded into background.

"Sorry to put you on the spot with the whole

boyfriend thing earlier. I hoped you would say yes." His lips were close to her ear again and a thousand needles pricked her skin.

Her smile got bigger. "It's been a long time since I had a boyfriend. I hope I don't screw it up."

"That makes two of us. I care for you very much, Liz." His breath came out in a rush. "There, I said it and I've had no alcohol or drugs to speak of."

"I like you very much, too." She made herself maintain eye contact even though her instinct was to look away. He could be so intense.

Liz heard something behind Ian and looked around him. "Uh-oh." She started unbuttoning her shirt. "Johnny and Paul are taking their clothes off. I think we're the target."

She threw her shirt on the ground and unbuttoned her jeans while Ian stood staring.

"If you don't want to get thrown in the pool fully clothed, I suggest you shuck something off." She jumped in the pool before they got her. She surfaced to see a shirtless Ian with her two youngest brothers on either side.

"You get him," Paul said.

"Uh-uh, you get him," Johnny said.

Meanwhile, Ian kicked his shoes off and dropped his jeans to reveal boxers.

"Honey, he's a boxer's man. I told you." Paul nodded to his wife.

"I'm surprised he bothers with underwear at all," Johnny said.

While they debated the merits of boxers verses briefs verses commando, Ian jumped into the pool himself. Her brothers cannonballed in right behind him.

"I think it was your big guns that scared them off," Liz said.

"I'm sorry, my big what?"

"Guns, you know." She squeezed his bicep.

"Good. I wasn't sure I could take them both at once."

The rest of the adults changed into swimwear and joined the pool party. Liz was thankful she'd worn a tank top under her button down shirt.

They played water volleyball and the kids joined in the fun. The little ones loved getting picked up by Ian and her brothers because the men were so tall. In the end, the younger kids were on the guys' shoulders. The only thing that made it fair was the little ones had bad aim. The older kids did a lot of getting out of the pool to chase the ball.

When they got out and dried off, Katie gave them robes to wear while she put their clothes in the dryer. Liz was very aware of her state of undress as she watched Ian do his thing onscreen.

After the show, her brothers teased Ian mercilessly, but he took it all in good fun. As she walked out of the room to get their dry clothes, Johnny said, "They named your character Dr. Duncan because he's always dunkin' his doughnut in some nurse's coffee."

She was folding Ian's boxers when he came into the laundry room. He grabbed the belt of her robe and pulled her closer. The kiss he laid on her then wasn't soft or sweet. It was pure passion. When he pulled away, they were both panting.

"I'm trying to behave myself." He pushed aside the collar of her robe and kissed a line along her clavicle leaving a trail of fire.

Every nerve ending tingled at his touch.

"If this is you behaving then, *Please sir, I want some more.*" She gave him her best Oliver Twist impersonation.

He laughed before he kissed her again and backed her up against the dryer. There was a knock at the door. *Of course.*

Danny poked his head in and back out again. "Sorry to interrupt. Lizabelle, Mama D is looking for you."

Ian stepped away and bent to pick his boxers up off the floor. She grabbed her clothes and they went to separate bathrooms to dress.

"Liz, I wondered if you and Ian would ride out to Southland in the morning to pick up a few things for me. I left in such a hurry. I've already called May and she'll have some clothes packed for me." Her mom stood by the kitchen counter.

"It'll get you guys away from the press for a few hours and who knows, maybe they'll get bored and go away," Danny said.

Jason, who had left for home after the show, walked in. "Hey, there are photographers at the end of the driveway."

"They must've figured out Robert and Katie were part of the crew," Danny said. "Jason, will you take Liz in your truck and go the long way around back to her house? Ian and I will follow you out and go the opposite way. That'll make it harder to tail us."

"Evasion. I dig it, bro." Jason looked excited about getting to participate in Operation Avoid the Press.

Ian, on the other hand, didn't look thrilled. Liz

assumed it was because she'd be with Jason.

She put her arms around Ian's waist. "I'll see you back at the house in a bit." She gave him a quick kiss on the lips and followed Jason to his truck.

***

"Are you doing okay with all this, Lizabelle?" Jason held her door open.

"I guess so. The anticipation is a little stressful, but I'm trying to accept it. It's part of the package." She lay down in the fetal position in the seat of the truck.

Jason slid behind the wheel, grabbed a sweatshirt from the back and made a pillow for her. "Liz, I hope you know what you're doing."

"I have no idea what I'm doing, Jason. Maybe this is going to really be something."

"Or, it might crash and burn."

"You don't wish that for me, do you?" She looked up at him and guilt swamped her. She'd wished it for him and it happened.

"I don't wish you any harm or heartache. I already caused you more than anyone should ever have to endure. It's just that you and Ian are from different worlds. You live over two thousand miles apart. I don't see him doing the adapting, I see you doing it all. If you think he's worth it, then by all means, go for it. But think about it before you get in too deep. You have to give up some things for his lifestyle."

Jason knew exactly how to hit her where it hurt. She liked being ordinary nowadays. She wasn't like that before, when her career had been her life, but that changed when she sold her software. She'd gotten some recognition at the time and took steps to become anonymous. If she hadn't, then she'd always wonder about people's motives—if they liked her for her or what she could give them.

"You can sit up now, we weren't followed."

She let out a breath. "I don't know, Jason, maybe I can be the closet girlfriend."

"You think he'll want to hide you under a rock while he flies solo?"

"No, I think he'll want me by his side."

"That says a lot about his feelings for you."

"And my willingness to do it or not says a lot about my feelings, right?"

Jason answered in the affirmative while Liz thought about what she'd be willing to give up to be Ian's girlfriend. So far it hadn't seemed like a huge sacrifice. She leaned her head against the window and closed her eyes.

When she opened them, she was home and Jason was opening her door. She covered her mouth and yawned.

"Come on, sleepyhead. Let's get you inside." Jason took her hand and helped her out of the truck.

She concentrated on putting one foot in front of the other while Jason guided her into the house.

"Unless you need my help getting up the stairs, I'll leave you to it."

She yawned again and hugged him. "Thanks, Jase."

He was about to kiss her cheek when the door to the kitchen opened. She turned her head and Jason's lips landed on hers. She was too shocked to move for what felt like a full minute, but it was only two seconds. She stepped back as Ian cross his arms over his chest.

"It's not what it looks like." She yawned again.

"Get to bed, Lizabelle." Jason pushed her toward

Ian and left.

"It really…that was an accident. He was aiming for my cheek but...the door and...my head." Her jaw cracked during the yawn and she rubbed the spot with her fingers.

"I guess it's only fair since you watched me kiss another woman on the telly tonight."

"That's your job," she said as she walked past him into the kitchen.

"Jason gets a goodnight hug and I don't?"

"Are you jealous? Because, I thought you were sleeping in my bed tonight."

"In that case, I'm no longer envious." He followed her down the hall.

Ian changed clothes and performed his evening hygiene routine in the guest bath so Liz could use hers. She was too tired to do anything but brush her teeth, then she kicked her shoes off and fell into bed fully clothed.

When Ian turned off the lamp and slid into bed beside her, she smiled despite her fatigue. Without a doubt, he'd be a better bedfellow than Nick.

"Come here, my love." He tugged and she army crawled until her head rested on his chest.

"I hope you weren't embarrassed earlier when your brother walked in on us."

She grunted. "It could've been my mom."

Ian shivered. "I shouldn't have done that there, I'm sorry."

"Oh, hey Mama, Ian's just rehearsing a scene." She shook with a silent laugh.

"Then the whole family would be at the door watching." He squeezed her shoulder. "Liz, I'm going to let you take the lead on the physical aspect of our relationship. You're going through quite a lot emotionally right now with your father. I don't want you to have any regrets about us."

A wave of gratitude rolled through her as she gave him another piece of her heart. "Thank you. It really means a lot to hear you say that."

He smoothed her hair and placed a kiss on her head. For a moment, she relished the security of his embrace before sleep pulled her under.

CHAPTER TWENTY-THREE

The next morning, there was a light knock on the bedroom door before Danny stuck his head in. Ian thought he'd learn not to do that.

"Hey, I'm going downstairs to work out if you'd care to join me. I could use a spot."

"Sure." He eased his arm from under Liz and she rolled onto her side.

"Y'all work out for me while you're at it."

An hour later, they returned upstairs to find Liz rolling up her yoga mat.

"I wish I'd seen you practice." Ian took in her fitted tights and tank. "Liz Baker, you're making it very difficult for me to keep my hands off you."

"Well, I certainly don't want to make your life difficult." She winked.

Danny cleared his throat. "If you two could focus on something besides each other for a moment, I'm planning to be at the hospital today. Call me when y'all get back from Southland and I'll come here to pick you up and take you through the secured entrance."

Ian paid attention to road signs as Liz drove to Southland. He wanted to learn the way. The further they got from the city, the more wooded and rural the landscape became.

Liz turned down the radio. "Can I ask you about something?"

"Of course." He turned toward her.

"You've not really told me about Emma. What happened between you?" She glanced his way.

He sighed. "When I moved to America and first got the role on Trauma, my agent suggested I find a high profile woman to date. She needed to be someone the paparazzi frequently followed because it would get my face into circulation. It worked because soon, everyone in Hollywood knew my name by association with her."

"She's British, right?" Liz asked, eyes ahead.

He pressed his palms onto his knees. "Yes, and initially it was nice to spend time with someone from home. But, Emma is even more ambitious than I am and...she isn't a very nice person. I mean, she was nice to me until I refused to bow to her wishes. The only reason she didn't malign me in the press when we broke up was because I broke it off with her unexpectedly."

"Oh?" Liz raised her eyebrows.

"I learned from Mum that Emma expected me to propose last Christmas. My family believed she could convince me to have children and since that's what they want for me, they supported her efforts. When they ganged up on me to let me know what was expected, I lost my temper with them." He looked out the window.

"My agent was furious because he expected backlash from the media. When our breakup only received brief attention which was positive for me, he let it go." He shrugged.

"What does your agent have to say about you dating me?" She took her eyes off the road to look at him for a moment.

Ian wasn't about to tell her the truth and risk hurting her feelings. She had enough to fret over.

He kept his expression neutral. "Not much. He said we looked great together at the premiere. There really hasn't been other press about us. I'm sure I'll hear from him if something comes up."

"So, he has a lot of influence over your decisions?" Her eyes were back on the road.

Ian wasn't sure if it was a question or a statement. Either way, it put him on the defensive.

He angled his body toward her. "Over my career decisions, yes, but he doesn't control me, he merely makes suggestions which benefit my career."

They pulled into a drive with an enormous wrought iron gate. The sign read: SOUTHLAND.

"Welcome to Southland," she said as they waited for the gate to open.

Both sides of the drive near the road were wooded. About a quarter mile in, the left side opened to fenced pastureland where several horses grazed. The packed dirt driveway continued to curve around trees and through the forest for nearly a kilometer until it opened to the main house.

Ian's jaw dropped at the sight of the colossal mansion. It was a two-story home of log and stone with massive stone columns. It resembled some of the grander lodges he'd visited. The oversized double front doors were polished wood and glass. The windows on the lower level were also oversized.

The drive circled in front and split around the house in both directions. Liz stayed to the right and passed a six car garage with carriage style doors. There was a covered breezeway connecting the house and garage.

Liz parked the car and they both got out. The back of the house had a porch running its width, complete with rocking chairs and two hanging swings. Centered behind the house was a half-Olympic sized pool with a slide and diving board. On one end, steps led out of the pool to a twelve person hot tub. Steps led down from there to a smaller, shallower pool.

"That one's for the younger kids until they can swim in the big pool," Liz explained when she saw him examining the area. "It also helps to keep pee out of the big pool. Although with my brothers, one can never be sure."

An elderly black man approached and Liz hugged him. "Hey, Uncle Ben Hill."

"Is this your special someone, Lizabelle?" He gestured to Ian.

"Yes sir, this is Ian. He's the one I went to the premiere with."

"Well, don't that beat all? We looked at those pictures on dat computer. Y'all sure looked fancy, all dressed up."

"Thank you." She smiled.

Ian extended his hand to Mr. Ben Hill. "It's a pleasure to meet you. Liz speaks very highly of you and Miss May."

"Yeah, she one of our many chirren." He ruffled her hair. "May's in there making y'all some lunch. I'm 'bout to go move some feed sacks, then I'll be in there to eat."

"Could you use some help?" Ian asked.

"You betcha. Johnny usually stay out here and help me with the heavy lifting, but with Big Dan in the hospital, I know how it is. He gone be alright though, Lizabelle." He patted her arm.

"I think so, too." She gave Ben Hill a kiss on the cheek and Ian got one, too. "Thanks for helping him."

Ian smiled as she went in the back door of the house. He subconsciously rubbed his side. He was a lucky man. Not only was there something special about Liz, there was something special about her family and her home. For a moment, he imagined a quiet life with her. He pushed the thought aside because it was so foreign to his way of thinking, so not in line with his goals, it didn't belong.

***

Liz helped Aunt May with lunch. When the guys came in to eat, they were hot and sweaty.

Liz handed Ian a glass of iced tea with a warning. "Take a small sip, they call it sweet tea, but you and I might call it syrup."

He took a taste and she could tell it affected him like it did her. It made her jaws ache at first. In cutting calories, she'd learned to drink her tea with a lot less sugar. But, the older generation at Southland still thought the sweeter, the better. It was no surprise they were borderline diabetics.

After lunch, Liz gathered her mama's things and hugged Aunt May and Uncle Ben Hill goodbye.

Ian followed her to the driver's door. "I'd like to give it a go, if you don't mind. I need to learn my way 'round."

Liz's heart was happy. It sounded like Ian planned to stick around for a while.

"Okay, but you do know we drive on the right side of the road here in America?"

"It's the wrong side, but I think I can figure it out. After all, they gave me a driver's license in California."

"They'll give anybody one of those."

Liz was impressed because Ian drove most of the way to her house without needing her to direct him. *He's a keeper*. She believed it deep down, but they still had some hurdles to get over.

CHAPTER TWENTY-FOUR

Big Daddy had been moved to a private room on the cardiac floor, conveniently located next to the stairwell. It was good for easy in and out, as well as the crowd of visitors. Katie worked out a schedule so they could each spend a few hours every day and accommodate other visitors.

Liz, Ian, and Danny climbed the four flights of stairs. The closer they got to the fourth floor, the more nervous Liz got about Ian meeting her dad. Jason was the only serious boyfriend she'd ever brought home, but technically he'd been there first. She trusted her dad would be as accepting as the rest of her family had been.

"There's my Lizabelle," Big Daddy said when she walked in. "I was afraid you didn't want to see me."

"You know better." She kissed his cheek. "You're looking good for an old guy with a hole in his chest cavity."

"Talk to me when you're sixty-something. Is that your celebrity boyfriend everybody's talking 'bout?" Her dad nodded toward Ian.

"Yes, Sir. Let me introduce you."

The men shook hands.

"I'd give you a firmer handshake, son, but I don't want to pop this IV loose. They tell me you haven't left her side. I appreciate you looking after my girl."

"It's my pleasure, Sir." He put his arm around Liz's shoulders.

"You'll also appreciate that he helped Uncle Ben Hill move feed sacks in the barn today," Liz bragged.

"Two work outs in one day?" Danny flexed and patted his shoulders. "I'm still feeling this morning's session."

"I was glad to help. Apart from entertaining Liz, I haven't felt very useful."

"I appreciate it, man," Johnny said. "The hay's getting delivered Wednesday. If the paparazzi are still hounding you, maybe y'all can go back out to Southland."

"Yeah, I want May to bake me a pie and you can bring it when you come back," Big Daddy said.

"I'm not sure pie is on your heart healthy diet, Daddy," Katie said.

"If I hadn't just met this young man," Big Daddy gestured to Ian, "I'd tell you what I think of that diet."

"No need to hold back, Dad," Johnny said. "Ian's practically family."

"Lawd, y'all gone run him off," Liz said.

"It'll take more than that to send me running, love." Ian squeezed her arm.

After dinner at Katie's again, Liz and Ian got back to her house a little before nine o'clock. They'd just gotten inside when there was a knock at the back door. Liz opened it to find her neighbors, Susan and Pete. Susan held up a bottle of wine.

"Grab some glasses and let's sit out here and talk, girlfriend." Susan nodded to the wicker chairs and loveseat adorning the deck.

Liz got glasses and went out with Ian. She made the introductions and then told them about her dad.

"Did you get a delivery today?" Susan asked. "I saw a van this afternoon."

"I haven't been on the front porch."

Ian rose. "I'll check for you."

He came back carrying a gift basket. She glanced at the card and put it under her leg to read later. It was from Chris Ross.

"Nice basket," Pete said. "Is that Jasper Hill Shiraz?"

"Yes."

"That's over a hundred dollars a bottle and it's really good. If you ever want to share with your lowly neighbors..."

"Lowly my behind, now I know what to get you for Christmas," she said. Pete owned a large residential cleaning company with franchises in most of the Southern states. "Let's have a taste."

In addition to the wine and assorted chocolates (Chris knew how to cheer a girl up), the basket included a two hundred dollar gift card to *Ray's In The City*. Liz blinked at the number, thinking she misread. It was probably twenty dollars. She read the card in which he wrote that he knew two hundred was too little to feed her entire family, especially her brothers.

"Who's it from?" Susan asked.

Liz looked for Ian's reaction when she answered.

He smirked before he proceeded to tell them about her long-time crush and how Chris had recently moved back to town.

"Sounds like you have some competition, my man." Pete clinked Ian's glass.

"Between Chris Ross and her ex-husband, I do have my work cut out for me."

"I can't believe he spent over three hundred dollars," Susan said. "What's he do for a living?"

"He's an executive with a tech firm," Liz said. "I forget which one."

"So, you two have a geek connection?" Ian asked.

"No, he's business/marketing or something, MBA guy." She knew exactly, but didn't want Ian to think it mattered to her.

Danny arrived and joined them for a drink. While they visited, Danny made Pete and Susan aware of the possible press problem. They promised to keep an eye out.

When they stood to leave, Susan hugged Liz. "Let us know if you need anything that we can take care of."

"Thank you." Liz squeezed her arm. "Actually, could you get a crew out here Wednesday to clean my house? I know it's early, but I've had a lot of people in and out. Ian and I will be at Southland overnight."

"Consider it done, my friend." Susan stood aside as Pete kissed Liz's cheek, then shook hands with Danny and Ian.

Once inside, Ian helped Liz clean the wine glasses while Danny read the card from Chris.

"I guess Katie and Robert have been spending a lot to feed us all," Danny said.

Liz shook her head. "I gave Rosa my credit card Sunday."

"Good girl," Danny said. "Where's the receipt? I'll go halfsies with you."

"I'd like to get in on that action," Ian said.

"No," she and Danny said in unison.

"You're a guest," Danny said.

"But I haven't contributed anything since I arrived. Liz wouldn't even let me put gas in her car."

Liz took his hand. "If I went to visit your family, would they let me buy my own food or their gas?"

He shook his head. "Are you going to come with me to visit my family? They're eager to meet you."

"Let's see how it goes with Big Daddy."

"Of course." Ian kissed her lips. "I'm going to lie down. You two haven't had much time to chat lately. I'll see you in there."

"Wow, he wants to take you home to meet the family," Danny said when Ian had gone. "This sounds serious."

"Don't play like this wasn't what you hoped for all along."

"It's got nothing to do with me, Lizabelle...but I do like seeing you happy."

"Me, too." She smiled her cheesiest grin. "What should I do about Chris?"

"Hmm, good question. I think you should call him or maybe go see him. Tell him you and Ian have very recently become an item and offer to return the gift card. Tell him you drank the wine and it was delicious. Or buy a replacement bottle."

"He served me that wine years ago on one of our three dates. I got drunk and threw myself at him, but he was too much of a gentleman to take advantage of me."

"He likes his women awake or at least semi-conscious?"

"Don't you?"

"Oh yeah."

Liz massaged her temples. "I'll call him in the morning and see if he can meet me for lunch. Will you take Ian with you and I'll meet up with y'all after?"

When she got to bed, Ian was already asleep. She curled up next to him, rested her head on her pillow, and watched him for a while. Going to England to meet his family did sound serious. They needed to discuss where their romance was headed before it ended up as a summer fling with him leaving to work in L.A. and her staying home alone and single. The longer she was with Ian, the greater the risk of discovery. She liked doing good things in secret, like Batman in a pickup truck, but without the cape or the crime.

CHAPTER TWENTY-FIVE

Ian was not happy to be informed of Liz's plans to meet Chris for lunch. He understood, but he didn't like it. He particularly didn't like that she'd be on her own.

She and Danny had decided the press wanted photos of him, so they wouldn't bother her if she were alone. He secretly believed they were right, but he didn't want to risk Liz getting cornered without him to shield her.

Liz called Chris to schedule lunch. They agreed to meet at noon, but he might be a few minutes late if his meeting ran over.

While she got ready, Ian expressed his concerns to Danny. "What are we going to do while she has lunch?"

"Tail her."

"I like the way you think, mate."

They followed Liz to a Tapas Bar at Phipps Plaza.

"Why didn't we just drive her?" Ian asked.

"She wouldn't have gone for it."

"And if she finds out we've followed her?"

"Let's hope she doesn't." Danny pulled out a small pair of high powered binoculars. "This is probably overkill."

Danny shared the binoculars, but at fifteen after, Liz was still sitting alone.

"Wait," Ian said. "The woman speaking to Liz looks remarkably like Johnny's ex-wife."

"Let me see." Danny took the binoculars. "Dagnabit, this could be bad."

He grabbed his phone and told Ian to check social media sights. Within ten minutes, Tiffany had posted on three different outlets that Ian Clarke's girlfriend was at Twist.

"What do we do?" Ian asked.

"Wait. Let's see if anyone shows up."

Fifteen minutes later, a man sat two seats down from where Liz waited at the bar.

Danny called her and put it on speaker. "How's it going, Lizabelle?"

"Fine. Chris messaged me. His meeting's running later than he thought. He asked if I could wait a little longer. Where are you guys?"

"Out and about. I forgot to tell you I put a tracking bug in your purse in case you get in trouble."

"What? A bug? Is it a cockroach?" She snorted as she reached into her bag. "Is it on?"

"No, you have to activate it. That's what I was calling to tell you. It looks like a pen. It's in the outside pocket of your purse. Just click the end to activate it."

"What will happen if I do? Will a grappling hook target the front door so I can zipline to the exit and kick some people in the teeth on the way?"

"You've seen too many spy movies."

"Ooh, Ian could be the next James Bond. If Daniel

Craig would give it up. Oh…except for the Bond girls. Never mind. Don't tell him I suggested it."

Ian covered his mouth to conceal his laughter.

"Focus, Liz. The device will send an alert to my phone and I'll be able to hear you and track you. If it sounds like you're in trouble, I'll come get you."

"All righty then. The guy next to me is eyeballing me. Could he be trouble?"

"Maybe, trust your gut. If he says anything that sounds off, use the device."

They took turns watching through the binoculars as the man conversed with Liz. A couple of minutes passed before Danny's phone beeped. He pressed a button and they could hear Liz.

"If I were in Italy, I wouldn't think twice about having a glass of wine with lunch. It's funny how societal norms dictate personal choices," Liz said.

"Have you ever been to England?" The man asked.

"No, it's too rainy there. I like sunshine."

"California has a lot of sunshine." The man sipped his drink.

"I know, I've been there."

"How do you like Los Angeles?" The man asked.

"I've not spent a lot of time there, but I love San Diego and Santa Barbara." Liz played with her phone.

"I only ask about Los Angeles because I think I might have seen you there."

"Oh, I get that a lot. Usually people guess Gina Davis because of the hair, but she's six feet tall, can you believe that?"

"I thought I saw you at a premiere a few weeks ago."

Liz's ringtone played. "That's my lunch date calling.

Excuse me."

"Is it Ian?" The man asked as she answered her phone.

"Hey Chris...I understand...no, a rain check will be fine...okay, I'll talk to you later."

Danny shoved his phone into Ian's free hand. "Stay here. I'm going to get her."

"My lunch date couldn't get away from work," Liz said. "I guess I'll be going. Nice talking with you."

Ian watched through the binoculars as Danny got between Liz and the reporter and guided her out the door. If the man made a reply, the bug hadn't picked it up. Ian's own phone rang and he hit ignore when he saw it was his agent.

Danny shut Liz into the back seat of her SUV and drove away.

"What about my truck?" She asked.

"We'll come back for it," Danny said.

"You made it here awfully fast, brother mine. Were you just sitting out here waiting for some action?"

"Tiffany posted where you were online. It was only a matter of time until a reporter showed up," Danny said. "What tipped you off?"

"He offered to buy me a drink and I told him it wasn't five o'clock yet. He said it was almost five in England and I panicked."

"You did the right thing," Danny said.

"Are you all right, love?" Ian reached his hand back to her.

She squeezed it. "Yeah, but I want to punch Tiffany in the face."

"I'd like to see that." Danny smirked. "Let's go see Dad instead."

Later that evening at Katie's, Ian assisted as Liz made cookies for her nieces and nephews. They sang and danced around the kitchen to songs on the radio. She was fantastic with the children and they clearly adored her. It was a shame she couldn't have her own family.

"Cookie?" She offered. "Sorry, I meant to say *biscuit*?"

He took the warm biscuit from her and gave her a quick kiss before he bit down and moaned. "So good."

After he licked his fingers clean, he sat on a kitchen chair and tugged Liz onto his lap while the kids continued to twirl.

"This is one of my favorite things." She put an arm around his shoulders. "When kids sing and laugh and dance like no one's watching."

He embraced her more tightly and kissed her cheek. In his mind, he saw a long life filled with the love of Liz and the laughter of his children. The thought made him blink, but he didn't push it away this time. Maybe there was a way he could have it all *and* give her what she always wanted.

He thought of something he could do for Liz, but he was going to need help. He tried to decide which brother would be willing to help him and keep their mouth shut. Johnny was ruled out immediately and Danny would be wherever he and Liz were, so that left Paul.

CHAPTER TWENTY-SIX

The next morning as Liz and Ian were getting ready to go to Southland, she was surprised when Paul came in the back door with his kids, Carly and Tyler.

"Doughnuts, Aunt Lizabelle." Carly slid the box onto the counter.

"They're still warm," Paul said.

"Yum." Liz took Tyler from Paul's arms. "Do you guys want milk to go with your doughnuts?"

"Yes, Ma'am," Carly said and Tyler repeated like two-year olds do when learning to talk.

Ian came into the kitchen followed by Danny. Both were excited about breakfast.

After Ian had eaten two, he stood. "Liz, I'm going to put my luggage in the back of your SUV. I hope you don't mind that I'm bringing all of it, but with the housekeepers coming, I want to be cautious."

"You afraid someone might steal your underwear?" Danny asked around a mouthful of doughnut.

"You'd be surprised. In London, one of my housekeepers actually put her knickers in the drawer with mine. Talk about unsanitary."

As they were about to leave, Danny shook his head

at his phone. "Big Daddy says don't forget his pie."

Liz grinned. "The doctors are gonna kick him out of the hospital."

"That's likely part of his plan." Ian winked.

Ian drove them to Southland and didn't get lost. Liz told him how impressed she was and started to open the back to get her overnight bag.

"I'll get it in a bit, love. If we bring our things in now, we'll have to put them in separate rooms and move them later. I don't want to raise a question about your virtue with Miss May and Mr. Ben Hill."

"You're so thoughtful to protect my virtue." She gave him a quick peck.

They were going to be alone that night for the first time when one of them wasn't slightly incapacitated. She planned to institute the no cell phone rule. An image of a trail of clothes littering the floor flashed in her mind. Of course, she blushed right after she thought it.

Ian caught her chin in his grasp. "Impure thoughts?"

"It's all this talk about virtue. Come on, you have hay to haul and I have pies to help make."

After dinner, when the older couple had gone home to their cottage for the evening, Ian hugged her from behind. "Do you feel like taking a walk with me? Several people have mentioned the lake here at Southland. I'd like to see it under this full moon."

"I'd love to." She tossed her cell onto the dining table.

He did the same and held her hand as they walked the dirt path leading to the lake. When they exited the wood near the lake, Liz froze. It took a moment for her brain to register what she was seeing. Out on the dock, there were a few dozen LED candles flickering.

"Ian?" Her heart beat harder.

"I wanted to surprise you." He led her out onto the dock.

There was a blanket spread across the end of the dock. Soft music finished the mood that the lilies and wine set.

"You've been a busy boy." *It's on.*

"I hope you like it, but don't feel pressured. What I said about following your lead still stands."

"It's very romantic. Let's have some wine and see where we go." She wriggled her eyebrows.

They kicked off their shoes and hung their feet over the edge of the dock. They sipped the wine from plastic, stemless glasses.

"You've thought of everything." She leaned into him, resting her head on his shoulder.

"I had help."

The full moon on the smooth water's surface was a perfect mirror image of the sky above. Nature's shades of blue and gray combined to form a similarity to the sweetest eyes she'd ever seen. She turned to look into them.

Ian set his glass down and took her hand. "Dance with me."

Under a Georgia moon, they danced, bodies pressed together. A soft kiss turned into a passion filled frenzy of clothes flying in every direction. The heat of the July night was nothing compared to what they were putting out. In the few coherent thoughts which flew through her mind, she was glad the lake was nearby in the event they started a fire.

Liz didn't think she could wait another second to take their relationship to the next level and when he lay her down on the blanket, she didn't have to. The connections they'd been making became fully realized as an overwhelming sense of completeness filled her.

Afterward, they lay there, allowing their breathing to return to normal, and Liz had to wipe her eyes.

He propped on his elbow. "What's the matter, my love?"

His concern was touching, but she couldn't explain what she was feeling without getting too deep. "Take my word for it, these are happy tears," she said with a sniff.

He covered them both with a thin blanket and kissed her temple. "It may be rather early for this, but I cannot help myself. Liz, I'm in love with you."

It was getting deep after all, in a good way. No waders required. Her heart might never beat the same again. She wanted to squeal, but instead she stroked his cheek and took a deep breath. "I hope you don't think I'd do what we just did with someone I didn't love."

His lips pressed into her hair. "I knew that about you early on."

"I guess you might like it if I said it directly instead of tiptoeing around the subject."

"You can just whisper in my ear if you're afraid anyone will hear."

"I don't care if the hoot owls hear that I love you, Ian." She kissed his smiling lips.

He squeezed her hip and yelled. "Woohoo!"

She agreed it was time to lighten things up. "What do you say to a swim?"

"I say, lead on."

They jumped off the end of the dock into the dark water. They laughed and splashed and frolicked until the water got close to boiling. Ian carried her out of the lake as if she weighed nothing at all.

He interlaced their fingers. "Let's dance."

She could tell he was slowing things down and that made her love him even more. "Well, we do have all night."

"We have many more nights, love."

A slow dance with her lover in the light of the full moon; Liz could write an entire song based on it. She was living a dream and she didn't want to wake up. She dreaded the moment when reality intruded.

***

Ian pulled Liz closer as a bird sang them awake. The sky was beginning to lighten. They were wrapped in blankets and each other.

He twisted her hair around his finger. "I don't want it to end."

"It was the perfect night."

"We can make it a perfect morning." His lips traced a path down her neck. Every morning would be perfect if he could wake up with her.

"Ian, I never want to leave here, but we better go."

"Right, we have horses to ride this morning."

With obvious effort, she stood, wrapped a blanket around her and bent to pick up her clothes. Ian was relieved none of them had landed in the water.

"Don't hide from me, Liz." He took the dress from her hand and tugged at the blanket.

"I'm not hiding, but it's not wise to be, how do you say it? Starkers—in the daylight. I might scare the

202

critters."

"Sod the animals, you're beautiful." He unwrapped the blanket and stood back. "Yep, gorgeous even in the light of day."

She scratched behind her ear—a habit he'd learned meant she was uncomfortable.

"Aunt May and Uncle Ben Hill get up early."

"Bollocks. I forgot about them." Indeed, he'd forgotten about everyone else in the world, but his Liz.

They returned to the main house and showered separately since May would probably be in the house very soon. After breakfast, they saddled two horses and set off for a ride.

He waited until they'd been riding a few minutes before he checked on her. "How are you feeling, love?"

"The song *Back in the Saddle* is playing in my head." She grinned. "I'm good. Better than good."

His smile had likely never been bigger. "I'm very happy to hear it."

They rode along a trail through the wood and came out by a creek they followed to the lake. Ian could see the dock in the distance. "I'll never be able to approach this spot without remembering last night."

"Me either, and I bring the kids out here swimming a lot. Now they'll wonder why my face turns bright red every time I step foot on the dock."

"We could find another place, if you think it would help?" He pressed his lips together.

"Have mercy."

He laughed.

She shook her head. "I think you're insatiable."

"No, I'm quite satisfied and quite in love." His heart

felt light yet full at the same time.

When they approached the barn, close to midday, Ian's heart sank when he saw a law enforcement vehicle. A man in a uniform was speaking with Ben Hill. Ian prayed nothing had happened to Big Dan. Liz would be devastated.

Ben Hill took their horses while Liz hugged the officer. Ian tried to reign in the envy gripping him. The man was the proverbial tall, dark, and handsome. And he'd clearly never seen a weight he couldn't lift.

"Is everything okay, Heath?" Liz asked.

"Danny's been trying to reach you," the man said. "It's *not* about Big Dan."

"Good." Liz let a sigh of relief and Ian did as well.

Ian stepped forward and extended his hand. "Ian Clarke."

"I'm sorry. Ian, this is Heath Cook. He's an old friend of Maddie's. They used to rodeo together."

"Nice to meet you, Ian. Danny hired me to help a little with security."

"Has something happened?" Ian asked.

"Apparently, the press knows where Liz lives now. Go call Danny." Heath gave her a push toward the house.

Ian had several missed calls from his agent, but before he rang him back, he wanted to hear what Danny had to say. Liz put him on speaker.

"Lizabelle, you need to keep your phone on you," Danny said.

"Why? What's up?"

"Only your and Ian's pictures are probably going viral as we speak."

Her eyes got wide. "They aren't nude photos are

they?"

"How would...why would...never mind. No, they're not."

Ian responded to her relieved smile by pulling her into his arms.

"Apparently, Ian was named one of the hottest Hollywood hunks or something. The media presence here has increased three-fold and they're staking out your house," Danny said.

Ian called his agent. The *Hottest Hunk* award came on the heels of the news that Ian got the lead in a romantic comedy opposite a big named actress. Filming would begin the following January. It looked like he was finally getting what he wanted professionally...and something he hadn't known he wanted personally.

"Ian, playing the dutiful boyfriend while her father is on his death bed is working out well for you."

Ian could practically see the smug look on Will's face. "I'm not pretending."

"You can't be in love with her."

"No, of course not." Ian couldn't admit it to his agent. It was a new feeling for him and he wanted to enjoy and explore it without judgment.

"Good, then you can use her to your advantage until it's time to move on. Get in front of the cameras. Get more shots like the one in the elevator of you comforting her. This is great buzz. You're on your way." Ian struggled to remember the shot and when he did, he smiled because Liz had been laughing, not crying.

Ian had a knot in his stomach by the time he disconnected. He needed to decide what he truly wanted and be ready to make a stand when the time came.

CHAPTER TWENTY-SEVEN

With Heath's escort, Ian drove them to meet Danny at Liz's house in Midtown. When they arrived and when they left for the hospital, cameramen got out of cars parked along the street. But they pressed on, because Liz had pie to deliver.

As they ascended the stairs to the fourth floor, they heard commotion above them. Danny and Heath took point and Ian put his arm around Liz. They waited on the landing between the second and third floors.

Two men in uniforms matching Heath's rounded the corner. Ian had learned they were Georgia State Patrolmen. Two men in suits followed the officers.

"Danny, Liz- there you are," one of the suited men said.

"Governor, good to see you." Danny shook the man's hand.

The governor introduced the other suit, who was his Public Relations Aide before he hugged Liz. "Lizzie, you look beautiful."

Ian tried to hide his smile, knowing Liz disliked the nickname. He thought he understood the reason why. It implied familiarity which the person clearly did not have.

"Governor Jenkins, let me introduce you to my friends, Ian Clarke and Trooper Heath Cook."

The Governor shook hands with both Ian and Heath. Ian loved that by Liz's introducing Heath, it forced the Governor to acknowledge his own security detail. She was a clever woman.

"I was just up to see Dan," the Governor said. "He looks good for a man who just had open heart surgery."

"Yes, Sir," Danny said. "We're very glad he's doing so well."

"As am I," the Governor said. "I'm glad we ran in to you all. My PR man hoped we'd meet with you, Liz and Ian, maybe get a photograph."

"I'm sure you don't want me in the shot," Liz said, then turned to Ian. "Are you okay with it?"

He agreed because he didn't see how he could decline and not be considered rude. They took one photo of Ian and the Governor and a second which added Liz. In the second shot, the Governor took his suit jacket off and loosened his tie, again implying familiarity. They said their thanks and farewells and continued on their way.

Once in the room, Liz let out a sigh of relief.

"You brought me two pies?" Big Dan's eyes lit up.

"No Daddy, one of them is for the nurses for having to put up with you." Liz kissed his cheek.

There were other visitors in the room and as Liz moved to greet them, Ian recognized Chris Ross. Liz hugged the older woman with him, his mother as she was later introduced. She also gave Chris a side hug, much less body contact than there'd been at the bar.

After the introductions, Mrs. Ross directed her stare at Ian. "I can see now why my son was nearly mauled at the hospital entrance. You two have similar height and coloring."

"What happened?" Liz asked.

Big Dan answered with a huge grin. "Apparently, the press thought Chris was Ian from a distance so when they started taking pictures, a bunch of fans crowded around for a look. If there weren't extra guards at the entrance, he might've been molested on the street."

"It was scary," Mrs. Ross said. "I don't know how you stand it."

"I kinda liked it," Chris said. "I got a few phone numbers and a ladies' undergarment shoved in my pocket. Mom made me throw it out."

Liz laughed. "Get your pants disinfected, just in case. I'm sorry that happened to you guys."

"You just missed the *man* himself," Big Dan said.

"No, we didn't," Liz and Danny said in unison.

They repeated the stairway encounter and after a moment Liz whispered to Ian, "I need to talk to Chris for a minute."

He reluctantly let go of her hand. He couldn't recall ever being so envious of other men in his life.

***

Liz picked up a pie box. "Chris, will you walk with me to deliver this to the nurse's station?"

"Sure." He held the door for her. "So this is why you wanted to meet for lunch, to tell me about your new boyfriend? My timing is always off with you."

"I also wanted to thank you for the gift basket and since you know about Ian now, I can return the gift card. It was very generous of you."

"Absolutely not, I've known your family forever. Keep it and feed them. I admit I was thinking of a possible date with you as incentive, but it's fine. I'm glad you have someone who makes you smile."

"I am happy, aside from the press. That stuff stresses me out. I feel like I always have to be on, ya know, like at any moment someone might pop out and take my picture."

As if she conjured it up, a man with a camera rounded the corner and began snapping photos. The nurse raised her voice at him and called for security. Liz tried to get past him to set the pie on the counter, but he wouldn't move. Chris stepped in front of her and suggested the cameraman back off. He was too polite.

The man spouted questions, but Liz couldn't concentrate on any of them. She leaned forward and put the pie box on the nurse's desk. The man's elbow knocked it to the floor because he was crowding her. Smoke came out of her ears.

She clenched her fists and pressed her lips into a tight line as she eased her right foot back to put her in fighting stance. As her mind raced to choose the best blow to deliver to put the man on his butt, she lifted her back knee and placed a solid front kick where the sun don't shine.

"You ruined my pie," she bit the words out as the man sank to his knees, dropping his camera in order to hold his crotch.

He made a squeaky noise and lay down on his side in the fetal position until two security guards arrived to help him up and out. Liz hadn't thought through the consequences of her actions, but when it was time to pay the reporter restitution, she'd have to hold on to the satisfaction of putting him down.

"Sorry about your pie, ladies." Chris picked up the upside down box and returned it to the counter.

When they opened the lid, the meringue was destroyed. Her vision blurred and she couldn't stop the tears. A nurse handed her a tissue and Chris put his arm around her to lead her back to Big Daddy's room.

They were almost there, when her cell phone buzzed. She would've ignored it, but it was her home security company.

"Miss Baker, this is Charles. The alarm was activated at your home. Do we need to send the police?"

Danny walked out of the hospital room on his phone. "Is that the security company?"

She nodded.

"It's Jason."

"Charles, my friend set off the alarm. I forgot he was coming by when I set it."

Danny motioned for her to give him the phone. "Charles, I'm gonna let you talk to my brother, Danny, he's on my account."

They traded phones.

"Jase, what are you doing at my house?"

"Danny told me the grass needed cutting and your lawn people weren't coming 'til next week. With the press and all, he thought the yard should at least look kempt."

"Thank you for that. When we left the house earlier, I panicked and set the alarm, knowing there were photographers prowling around. If I'd known you were coming, I'd have warned you."

"No problem, as long as the cops don't come pick me up."

"I owe you one."

"I was hoping you'd say that. I need you."

Uh-oh. She scratched her neck. "For what?"

"Sara is still out of town with her sick Grandma. I need you to play and sing with me tomorrow night."

"Uh, Jason." A whiney little girl's voice came out. She dropped her shoulders and sighed as she dabbed the corner of her eye with a tissue. "I'll need to talk to Danny and Ian and get back to you."

Liz turned off her phone. She did not need anything else on her plate at the moment. She loved Jason and loved to play music, but it was not a good time. She was distracted the rest of the evening until Ian took her to their alternate reality, the place where fairy tales come true.

CHAPTER TWENTY-EIGHT

When Liz awoke the next morning, she found Ian, Danny and Heath working out in her home gym. She should work out too, but sipping coffee and watching some well-muscled men seemed like a better use of her time. Ian in particular was causing her heart to sputter and body to warm from the inside out.

"You want to work in with us, Liz?" Heath asked.

She held her coffee cup to her lips. "I want Paul to show up with some Krispy Kremes."

Late morning, when Liz was almost dressed and ready, she heard raised voices in her living room. She went to check it out.

"What the hay, Lizabelle?" Jason yelled. "Are you just hoping I'll go away?"

Her chest tightened. "Ah, I forgot. Let's talk in here."

She went into her room and he followed her in and slammed the door.

"I'm sorry, Jase, but in case you missed it, I have a lot going on right now."

"Was a phone call too much to ask for?"

"I turned my phone off and forgot about it until I

heard you hollering."

"What's going on?" Danny asked from the doorway with Ian right behind him.

"I need Liz to play tonight and she was supposed to talk to you and get back to me." Jason rested a fist on his hip.

"The timing sucks on this, Jase," Danny said.

"I know, but I wouldn't ask if I had another choice. Without her, our set list is cut in half."

"I'll do it." Her stomach turned.

"Don't let him bully you into this," Danny said. "We need to talk about it. We can't control who comes in and out."

"Can I talk to Jason a minute?" Her heart was racing. "Please?"

Danny closed the door leaving Liz facing her ex-husband.

"Jason, I'm scared. Before this media stuff, it was fun...But now, I don't want people watching and judging my talent. I'm just an amateur and I like it that way."

"Lizabelle, you're one of the best guitar players I've ever met. And you have a beautiful voice. Please don't let him, I mean them, take this away from you." Jason held her hands. "I'm a little freaked out too. I sing and play for the same reasons you do. I love it, but it's not my day job. I don't expect any record deals. Let's just go out there and have fun like we always do."

Liz let out a long breath and dropped her head. Jason put his arms around her and she rested her forehead on his chest.

She closed her eyes. "I guess we need to go clear this with the chief of security."

"You could ask Ian to stay here tonight," Jason said.

"I'm not going to do that. If he doesn't want to go, that's one thing, but I'm not asking him to stay away." She opened the door and went to the living room where Ian, Danny and Heath were waiting.

"We're going to do this Danny, so figure it out." She sat next to Ian.

"Are you sure?" He asked.

"I'd like to know something." Ian's posture was stiff. "How can you have such an easy relationship with Jason after what he did to you?"

She looked at her hands. "I told you there were extenuating circumstances."

"You can tell him, Lizabelle," Jason said. "In fact, I'm surprised you haven't."

"It's not my story to tell. Plus, it would just sound like I'm making excuses for you."

"Well, I'll tell it. He has no right to be ticked off with you," Jason said.

"I'm not angry with Liz, I'm angry with you. I think you're manipulating her."

"How about I tell you a little story and you can judge for yourself? I don't care what you think of me, but if you think Liz is easy to manipulate, you've got another thing coming."

"Let's have it then," Ian said.

"What I say doesn't leave this room," Jason said.

"Understood," Ian said.

"I'll go." Heath stood.

"No, Heath, stay," Danny said. "You understand the need to know and you can judge whether you think Liz is too lenient on Jason."

"I don't want to do that." Heath sat back down.

"But I'll stay for the sake of an argument."

"I'm going to my room." Liz closed the bedroom door. Jason's story was heartbreaking and she couldn't hear it again.

**

Ian knew he was being a prat for asking for an explanation, but he needed to understand. Most of all, he wanted to know why Liz couldn't or wouldn't tell him.

"Years ago, I worked with a woman. She was a single mom and my buddy was interested in her. Long story short, we stopped by her house and walked in on a domestic situation. The girl's father had knocked the mom out and was kidnapping his daughter. She was about Carly's age." Jason clenched his fists.

"She had divorced him because he was molesting the little girl. We called the cops and she begged us to keep it quiet. She was new to town and didn't want anyone to find out for her daughter's sake." He stretched his fingers.

"I couldn't stand lying to Liz, so I started avoiding her. The little girl was precious and I guess she sort of saw me as a hero or something...her mom, too. My buddy lost interest and call it vanity, but it felt good to have someone look at me that way. Gradually, I started spending more and more time with them. One thing led to another and I cheated. It went on for a few months and when I was about to break it off because Liz and I were about to do some fertility stuff, she told me she was pregnant. The rest is history."

"You told me you had no children," Ian said, his voice still hard.

Jason ran his hand through his hair. "The baby was

stillborn and she blamed me. Said I brought it on us because I betrayed Liz. I guess I blamed myself, too." He hung his head.

"When did Liz find out the truth?" Ian asked.

"When I moved back here, about a year and a half ago." Jason leaned back on the sofa. "I know it's no excuse. I still hurt her, but I wanted her to know it wasn't her fault."

Contrition didn't sit well on Ian's shoulders. He couldn't imagine what he'd do if he were in Jason's shoes. "Thank you for telling me. I owe Liz an apology."

He went to her door and knocked lightly before entering. She was lying on the bed staring at the ceiling.

He sat next to her. "Do you regret falling in love with me yet?"

Her smile was a little sad. "I don't regret falling in love with Jason even though it turned out to be painful. Why would I regret loving you when all you've done is be a little jealous of my ex-husband? That's normal, isn't it?"

"How can you be so gracious?" He lay next to her and propped on his elbow.

"I guess I hope that when the day comes that I need grace, someone will be willing to extend it to me."

"You're far better than I deserve. I love you." He kissed her with the tenderness in his heart. "So, are you ready to sing your heart out tonight?"

"Are you going with me?" She sounded hopeful.

"There's no place I'd rather be. I can stay in the sound booth again, if that's all right. I don't want to be the cause of any trouble."

"I think we can work something out." She put her arms around his neck and kissed him.

If there weren't three men in the next room, he'd have his way with her. After a moment, it looked like she was going to have her way with him. And did she ever.

Half an hour later, they redressed and returned to the security planning party in the living room. Heath called in a few off duty troopers to help. The bar owners were informed of the situation and the added security Danny was supplying.

***

The evening passed without many glitches. Two television news crews were turned away at the door. Five men with large cameras were told they couldn't enter with the equipment.

After the bar emptied of patrons, Jason got the band to play one last song so Ian could dance with Liz. A picture of them dancing found its way online the next day.

Additionally, there were a few camera phone photos and one video of Liz and the band. The sound quality on the video stunk because of the ambient noise and that alleviated Liz's fear of a critique of her talent.

Ian loved one of the photos of Liz. In it, her eyes were closed, her mouth was open and both hands gripped the microphone stand. He smiled to himself because her guitar covered one of his favorite things; the lucky horseshoe belt buckle she wore.

Later, after closing her bedroom door, he traced the outline on the metal. "Do you feel particularly lucky this evening?"

Her smile lit up the dim room. "I'm the luckiest

woman in the world."

His heart melted at his good fortune to have found such an amazing partner.

***

Dan Baker was released from the hospital and much of the family went to Southland to stay. Ian drove Liz in her SUV. He'd never been so happy as they rode the back roads of Georgia. They opened the sunroof, rolled the windows down, turned the radio up and sang along.

At one point Liz turned down the radio. "I don't want to spoil your good mood, but I need to tell you something."

"I already know you love me. That's all I need to know." He laced their fingers together.

"I'm being serious."

"What do you want to discuss, love?" He kissed the back of her hand.

"Money."

"It's necessary. I have plenty for both of us."

"So do I," she said.

"Well, the matter's settled then. No more talk of serious things."

She smiled and his heart fluttered in his chest. She was still having this effect on him. It was definitely love.

They spent a week at Southland. Ian was quartered in the guest cottage near the lake, which was perfect for the nights Liz snuck out of the big house after everyone was in bed.

The kids were there, so during the day, they swam and rode horses. Ian kept imagining having a family with Liz. He stopped himself from mentioning adoption to her on several occasions. It was too soon to discuss children when they hadn't even discussed marriage. He could see where their relationship was going and he had no desire to reverse course.

With the help of Big Dan, he convinced Liz to accompany him to London for a family wedding. He only had eight weeks until he had to return to L.A. to start filming the next season of *Trauma*. He wanted to spend every moment with Liz.

CHAPTER TWENTY-NINE

When they got off the plane in London, the paparazzi waited for them outside the airport. They barely made it to their hired car through the crowd. Liz was stunned, but she didn't kick anyone in the privates. She expected it to be worse than in the States, but these photographers were much more aggressive than any she'd encountered and she didn't have Danny along to protect her. He planned to stay at Southland for another week; until Liz got back.

She did have Ian though, and his sheer size alone was enough to make people move aside. She stayed in his wake and let him lead her through the crowd.

The car took them to his parents' home outside town. It was gated and more secluded than his flat. He told her he hoped the reporters would move on and he could take her to his place in a few days.

His parents' home was a massive Tudor of stone covered with ivy. His mom was tall, thin, and elegant with shoulder length blond hair. His father, whose face she did recognize, was also tall, slim and handsome with close cut gray hair.

"We're thrilled to meet you at last, Elizabeth."

"Mum, she prefers Liz."

"I'm sorry dear. I didn't mean to offend."

"The only time anyone ever called me Elizabeth was when I was in trouble. It brings back bad memories, although it sounds nice when you say it, Mrs. Clarke."

"Please, call me Jacqueline."

"And call me Simon." Ian's father hugged her. "You're very welcome to our home."

"Ian, I'm putting you in the adjoining rooms. Liz, there's a shared bath connecting the rooms. I hope it will be to your liking."

"Yes ma'am, that'll be fine."

"I see what you mean about the Southern accent now, son." Simon put his arm around Ian. "Adorable."

Ian squeezed her shoulder. "I told you they'd love you."

"The rest of the children and grandchildren will be here for tea," Jacqueline said. "I apologize for unleashing them all on you at once, Liz, but they are eager to meet you."

Liz was reminded of Southland as the family started pouring in. Now she knew how poor Ian must have felt meeting her family at the hospital. The difference was she wasn't on her own turf and she struggled with feeling overwhelmed. The itching began. She was a fish out of the creek and this creek bank wasn't familiar.

The younger kids monopolized Ian by trying to climb him like a tree, just like he'd said. That left Liz exposed to a barrage of questions from his brother and sisters. She knew the most about Sylvie, so she naturally gravitated toward her. Sylvie had recently gone through a bad breakup from her partner.

Donna was the eldest and she and her husband, Edward, were both accountants. They had two girls and a boy. Liz made a connection with their son, Stephen, because he played guitar.

"I insisted Liz bring her guitar." Ian hefted a kid onto one of his shoulders. "Perhaps, you can play together."

Collin was the third child, born right after Ian, and the only other son of the Clarkes. He and his wife Colleen also had three children, two boys and a girl name Katherine. Liz connected the name because of her own sister.

The fourth child was Brenda who was married to Daniel. Liz related not only to his name, but the fact that his career was in Information Technology, a field akin to her own. They had two kids, a boy and a girl.

At dinner, which they called tea, she was seated near Daniel and he asked too many questions about her job. The one thing she wanted least to talk about, he kept bringing up. She tried to give vague answers, but that only prompted more questions. She scratched her head and took larger sips of her wine to take the edge off.

"Where did you study?" Daniel asked.

Ian had never asked, not that it was a secret, but darn. She shook the thought away. "UGA and UC San Diego."

"Ian says you work in software. Are you in development?"

"I mostly do programming these days."

"What does that mean exactly?" Donna asked.

"Well, you work with accounting software,

correct?"

She nodded.

"The people who develop the software and write the code are often called programmers. And, you know how when you wish the software would do something it doesn't?"

"All the time. It would save me a lot of steps."

"When you make suggestions about it to the software developers, they have people who see if it's doable. If so, they write the code to upgrade the software and make it better. That's what I do."

"What discipline do you work in?" Daniel asked.

Go away, she thought, but her mind control powers seemed to be non-existent. She leaned to scratch her ankle, not wanting to answer him. She considered making up a story about working for a secret government agency, until she had the paranoid delusion that MI5 might come get her.

She struggled to maintain a pleasant expression. "I work in Health Informatics. Where did you study, Daniel?"

Once she got him talking about his own work, the questions about her work ended. Thank God. She should've thought to do that from the beginning, but she was out of her element. Dixie was calling her to come home, and she wasn't thinking about her mama.

When they went outside to enjoy a night cap, Ian pulled her to his side. "I saw what you did back there. Way to turn the conversation around, love."

Liz rubbed her knuckles on her thigh. She really wanted to tell Ian everything about her career. The last time she brought it up was to talk about the money. Maybe if she approached it from a career standpoint, he'd want to know. It struck her how they had always talked about his career and he never asked about hers. Maybe he didn't understand computers and didn't want to feel ignorant. Men hated that. But then, she'd been deliberately evasive early on. He might just be respecting her privacy. *Yeah.* That sounded better than he could care less.

Ian got her guitar while Stephen tuned his. The boy kept wiping his palms on his pants and she later learned he didn't play in front of people, not even his parents. Thankfully, he was a fan of some of the classic British artists and knew their songs. They played while the adults sang along.

"Just like home, huh?" Ian said from his place behind her on the chaise.

Not at all. But, she admitted to herself that hiding behind her guitar made her more at ease.

The little kids were getting bored so Liz played *Twinkle, Twinkle Little Star* and got them up dancing and singing.

"I never knew the singing, laughing, and dancing of the little ones was one of my favorite things until I met you," Ian said in her ear.

Liz's heart squeezed in her chest. Did Ian hold out hope of having kids of his own someday? He might change his mind, after his career was more established. The revelation came as a blow to Liz, because she'd convinced herself she didn't want them anymore. She questioned what she'd been doing for the past few weeks, involving herself with a man she had no future with.

"Liz, we're going shopping tomorrow for wedding attire." Sylvie gestured to her mom and sisters. "Get

Ian's credit card and we'll make it a girls' day."

"We'll have a game of golf. Men only." Simon winked at his wife.

***

"We'll take good care of her, Ian. Stop fretting," Donna said.

He insisted Liz take his credit card, which was why he was shocked to discover it in his wallet when they arrived at the golf club. He and his brother and dad played together while his brothers-in-law played behind them.

When they met up at the clubhouse for drinks later, everyone was already a bit blotto. Ian, remembering Liz, stopped drinking while the others continued.

"Ian, my good man." Daniel slapped his back. "You certainly know how to pick them. Pretty, off the charts clever and wealthy. She's the total package."

"Pardon?"

His father put an arm around him. "Yes, son, you better hold on to this one. If you want my advice, marry her and soon. You'll need to start working on a family right away because of her age? Tick-tock, old boy."

They toasted and cheered, but Ian didn't feel particularly joyous. He'd not told his family everything about Liz, especially the very personal information about her inability to conceive.

"I'm thinking about a trip to Harrods later," Ian said.

"Good for you, son." His dad hugged him.

He did go to Harrods and found a sapphire the same blue as Liz's eyes. It was surrounded by small channel set diamonds in the shape of a horseshoe. He took it back to his flat and hid it carefully. He hadn't worked out the details of the proposal yet, but he'd think of something. He wanted to be sure Liz was going to be all right with his lifestyle—cameras every time they turned around. He took her lack of complaints as a positive sign.

CHAPTER THIRTY

A few days after they arrived, Liz waved goodbye to his parents as Ian took her to his flat in London. They needed some alone time.

Ian took her on a tour of the city and for a ride on London's eye, complete with champagne. They were followed by cameramen from the time they left his flat until they returned. Although she loved Ian, she was getting tired of constantly dodging the press. It should be an Olympic event, because you certainly needed Olympic level conditioning to stay ahead of them.

One night, when they got back to his flat, they hadn't left a light on and since the switch was across the room, Ian left her near the door to go turn it on.

"My pet." Liz heard right before arms wrapped around her.

It wasn't Ian, so Liz wriggled out of their grasp before shoving the person away. The light came on as a scantily clad woman tripped backwards over an ottoman and fell onto the couch.

"Emma, what in God's name are you doing?" Ian helped her to her feet.

"I heard you were back in town." She patted her

hair. "I intended to surprise you. Didn't know you had your American whore in tow."

That was a lie because all of England knew Liz was in town with Ian.

Liz couldn't help herself. "If I were you, I'd get a refund on those." She pointed to where Emma's cleavage overflowed her silk nighty. "You could seriously hurt someone."

"These," Emma grabbed her breasts with both hands, "are for Ian, just like he got his nose done for me. Looks good, pet."

Liz tried not to look as shocked as she felt. She'd never asked Ian why he had his nose done, besides the deviated septum thing. "He wasn't good enough for you the way he was?"

"No...yes...argh..." Emma stomped her foot.

Liz made a mental note to never stomp her foot while her thighs were exposed. If it was unattractive on a woman with no body fat, it would definitely look bad if she tried it.

"Emma," Ian said. "Get your clothes and get out. And leave my key."

Emma went to the bathroom and dressed. When she walked past Ian, who stood holding the door open, she dropped the key at his feet.

"You haven't seen the last of me." Emma twitched her bony butt as she walked away.

"I'm sorry about that." Ian closed the door and leaned his head against it.

"Does that sort of thing happen a lot?"

"No."

Liz waited for him to elaborate, but he didn't. As her feelings for Ian grew, so did her insecurities.

That night was the first time Ian was unable to take her to another place, where she left reality behind while she was in his arms. She couldn't get Emma's perfect body out of her head.

When she reached down to pull up the sheet, Ian stopped her. "Don't even think about it, love."

While Ian slept, her mind raced. She wanted to go home, but she shouldn't leave before the wedding. His family expected her.

The tabloids had been running daily articles with pictures of them. She needed a break from the circus that was Ian's life. She didn't have what it took to handle the stress of the celebrity lifestyle. Her chest tightened to the point of pain. Leaving Ian would be impossible, but she couldn't think of a way to stay and not ask him to rearrange his priorities. She loved him too much to do that and she wanted him achieve his dreams.

***

The evening of the wedding arrived. Liz and Ian rode there in a limo with his parents. At the reception, Ian got a phone call from his agent. He excused himself to answer the call, but then he disappeared for a while. Liz was having flashbacks to the night of the premiere.

"Is something the matter, Liz?" Jacqueline asked.

"Oh, no. I'm just a little tired, I guess."

She started to tell Jacqueline she had an upset stomach, but that might prompt more questions. Her stomach trouble was because she was going to have to stop seeing Ian, or at least stop doing it so publicly.

She excused herself to the bathroom and while hiding out in the stall to catch her breath, she overheard an upsetting conversation.

"The paper said she's like a multi-millionaire or something and that Ian is only with her for the money," one woman said.

"That has to be it. Why else would he leave Emma? She's gorgeous," another woman said. "Don't get me wrong, the American is pretty, but she's no Emma, and we want Ian to end up with an Englishwoman, don't we? Not some wealthy American who'll steal him away and never let him come home."

"My boyfriend knows Emma and she told him Ian's only using the American. He plans to chuck her before he sends her back..." The voices trailed off as the ladies left the bathroom.

Liz dug her phone out of her bag and called Danny. "Something's rotten in Denmark. I might be coming home earlier than expected."

"You can smell Denmark from the U.K.? Are you a bloodhound?"

"Not laughing, bro." She explained what she'd heard.

"Lizabelle, don't leave without talking to Ian first. This could all be a misunderstanding."

"I hope it is, but I have a bad feeling."

Liz went in search of Ian. When she found him, he was half drunk. "We need to talk."

"It's a bit late for that, don't you think, Liz?"

"What's going on?"

"Are you trying to ruin my career?" His raised voice startled her.

The crowd around them quieted and turned to stare.

Heat crept up her neck and flooded her cheeks.

"Stop being so melodramatic and tell me what's happened, Ian."

She put a fist on her hip so she wouldn't put it through his handsome face. She'd been going through hell for him and he was making a scene.

"My agent called, and thanks to the reports in the press that I'm a moneygrubbing louse, I may lose my movie role. Thank you very much." He raised his glass to her.

"Ian, I didn't say anything to the press."

"Are you telling me that you didn't lie to me? Did you simply forget to tell me you sold the medical software you developed for the high seven figures?"

"I tried to tell you, but you didn't want to talk about it."

"Don't turn this around on me. I know how you work. You think you're so clever, don't you?"

She loosened her fingers then let them roll, one at a time, back into a fist. "I have tests to prove it, but that's beside the point. When have you ever shown any interest in my career? Oh, that's right. I remember now, we always talked about *your* career, which is the *most* important thing, isn't it Ian?"

"Yes, it is. Thanks for showing me who you really are, Liz Baker, before I did something stupid."

"So, this is how it ends. You're a real class act, Ian." She wanted to say something really hurtful, but couldn't bring herself to do it.

He pulled his keys out of his pocket and tossed them to Sylvie, who stood close by. In fact, all of Ian's family and many other onlookers were present to witness her downfall.

"Take her to get her things and drop her at the

airport."

"Ian, you can't mean it," his mom said.

"Get her away from me. I don't want to see her again. Ever." Despite his words, he kept his narrowed eyes on her.

Liz's body somehow managed to obey the hazy commands she gave it. Almost totally numb, she put one foot in front of the other. *Get out of here. He doesn't want you anymore.*

CHAPTER THIRTY-ONE

Ian's heart broke into tiny pieces as Liz trudged away. He wanted nothing more than to take her in his arms and kiss the devastated look from her face. With every step she took away from him, the crushing pain in his chest grew worse. He had to turn away. He wasn't strong enough to watch her walk out of his life.

She had lied to him and he was angry about it, but he wouldn't have let it tear them apart. If it weren't for his agent telling him he may lose the movie role he'd worked so hard to get, he'd run after her.

Will said they had to turn the bad publicity around. Ian needed to break up with Liz publicly and accuse her of lying and hiding her wealth from him. He also thought it would be a good idea for him to reconcile with Emma soon. Ian wasn't totally on board for either part of the plan, but he was unsure of the best course of action. This is what he paid his agent for, so he did as he was advised although it was painful. Apparently, fulfilling his lifelong fantasy of being the leading man meant giving up the woman of his dreams.

He stayed the night at his parents' home, even though they were vexed with him. He had to let them believe he was really done with Liz.

When he got back to his flat the next day, he secretly hoped she'd be there waiting for him. The only trace of her he found was her horseshoe belt buckle leaning against the mirror of his dresser. It was upside down, proving her luck had run out. In his heart, he knew his had too.

The message hit him in the gut and he sat immovable for an indeterminable length of time. When he thought about moving, his cheeks were damp with tears he hadn't realized he'd been crying.

This must have been what Jason felt when he let Liz go. He shook the thought away. He hadn't cheated on Liz. If anything, she'd cheated by lying to him.

A few days later, he renewed his relationship with Emma because the press was in favor of it. He didn't feel the things he ought to feel for her, but he was an actor. And he was getting better at it every day. He could hardly stand to look at his reflection in the mirror.

He didn't lose the movie role and just before he had to go back to Los Angeles to begin filming the next season of Trauma, Emma told him she was pregnant. He was incensed with her, but she insisted it was an accident. He didn't want to have children with Emma. If he had them with anyone, he wanted it to be with Liz.

At his agent's urging, he proposed. They were to get married quickly so he could get back to work. He threw up the morning of his wedding and told his mum he couldn't go through with it. He'd lost control of his personal life and was spiraling full speed down a dark hole.

"Ian, what's really going on?"

He told her about having to break up with Liz and how he still loved her and wanted to marry her, not Emma.

"Ring her," his mum insisted.

"She'll never take a call from me."

"What's her number?" She pulled her phone from her purse.

"Liz, this is Jacqueline Clarke, please don't hang up. Ian has something important to tell you and he was afraid you wouldn't take his call. Please, hear him out?"

"Liz." His voice was unsteady.

"Rumor has it you're going to be a father and a husband soon. Congratulations."

His heart raced. "It's not the way I wanted it, Liz."

"These things happen for a reason. Try not to worry and try to be happy. I wouldn't have been able to give you kids and I could tell by the way you adored your nieces and nephews that you hoped for them someday. Well, someday is here. Make the most of it."

"But...I...don't..." Words failed him.

"You'll make it work. You're a good man. You'll make a great dad. Best wishes. I have to go now."

"Liz..."

Nothing. The line was dead.

"Why didn't you tell her?" His mum asked.

Ian couldn't answer. All he could do was stand in stunned silence and all he could hear was his broken heart, struggling to beat.

***

Liz hung up the phone and thought back to the day she'd left London. Danny booked her flight to L.A.

through New York. She left from Gatwick instead of Heathrow, hoping to dodge the press. It didn't work and she had an incident with a reporter there.

He walked backward in front of her, snapping a thousand pictures. When she zigged, he did too. He tripped and fell, causing her to go down too. She wasn't too upset that her elbow landed on his windpipe, until he struggled to breathe. The nurse in her went to work until medics arrived.

Witnesses backed up the report she gave to security officers that it had been an accident. Many said he deserved it. She had delusions about being detained by British authorities until her plane was over half way across the pond.

Danny was still in Georgia, so he told her his business partner, Joe, would pick her up. It was afternoon when Liz landed at LAX. A woman named Jane said Joe from B&B sent her and took her to the ladies' room where she gave her a hat and sunglasses. With her hair in a ponytail, under a hat, no one noticed her. It helped that the press was expecting her in Atlanta.

She stayed at Danny's house by herself for two days until he sent Jason to get her and take her to Quiet Cove. She opened up to Jason, sharing her heartache with him. There were moments when guilt weighed on her, because she'd been thinking of breaking things off with Ian. She got what she thought she wanted, but she wished he'd handled it differently. Of course, Jason threatened to rearrange his face.

She told Jason about her financial situation since rumors were flying in the tabloids about it. He was aware of her trust fund and that she'd made a little money on her software, but he had no idea how much she was worth. It was kind of funny to watch the color drain from his face.

Jason didn't want to do it, but Liz put her hair in a ponytail at the top of her shoulders and he whacked it off with a pair of kitchen shears. He bought her a box of Clairol and she became blonde for the first time in her life. It amazed them both how much she looked like Katie.

Jason wanted to stay with her, but she didn't let him, knowing where it could lead. At that point, she had only allowed herself to be angry and a revenge affair might be something she was willing to try to make herself feel better. Going there with Jason would mean no turning back in his mind.

When the cameraman she'd kicked destroying a pie found out she was loaded, he brought a civil suit against her. Thankfully, since the man wasn't permanently damaged, the judge threw it out. It also didn't hurt that Big Daddy was a member of the good ole boys network and her Aunt Nancy was a darn good lawyer.

She enjoyed her condo in Quiet Cove and met with a contractor to start building her beach house. Danny came to keep her company and he bought the house next door, like he said he would.

She wrote a song called *Play With My Heart.* The chorus went:

When you play with fire, you're gonna get burned
Tornado blows through and your whole world's turned
Upside down and you don't know if it'll ever be right again

A hurt that only time can mend
Should've known right from the start
That you were gonna play with my heart

The title was inspired by something Jason said to her months before, though she'd never let him know about it. The song was strictly for her—so she could heal. At first, she sang it with an angry Alanis Morissette sound, but eventually it softened into the sad ballad it was.

She put back on the stress weight she'd lost while dating Ian and running from the paparazzi. The long, slow walks on the beach only made her hungrier. If it was chocolate, she was putting it in her mouth. She even found a chocolate flavored wine. That discovery reaffirmed her belief that God was looking out for her, although drinking too much of it made her sick. She deserved the treat after the humiliation of getting dumped in front of the world. Thankfully, the folks in Quiet Cove didn't seem to know or care about her broken heart.

CHAPTER THIRTY-TWO

Ian punched the wall by his back door. His six month sham of a marriage to Emma was over. Liz may have kept things from him, but she'd never outright lied and tricked him. Emma lied about being pregnant and then spent the next several months trying to get that way.

When she should've been showing and wasn't, Ian insisted on going to the doctor's appointment with her. That was when she *almost* told him the truth. First, she lied and told him she'd lost the baby and was too afraid to tell him. When he asked to speak to her doctor, the real truth came out.

He fired Will. He'd been interviewing another agent when he found out Will and Emma were friends from way back. Everything the arse advised him to do had been at Emma's urging.

Ian lost the best thing that had ever happened to him because of their lies and deceit and his own lack of a backbone. He picked up the phone to ring Liz several times, but kept hanging up. An apology wouldn't be enough this time. He wondered if Danny would take his call.

Ian almost hung up when he heard Danny's voice.

"Ian, hey, I thought you might call."

"I know I'm a total wanker, but I wondered if you hated me? And how Liz is doing?"

"I don't hate you, but I should. I hated Jason for a few years after he broke her heart."

"I'm so sorry, Danny. If I could take it all back I would, but I'm afraid there's too much water under the bridge."

"You might be right. I think Liz would agree at least."

"Honestly, the next time a woman tells me she's carrying my child, I'm going to demand a paternity test."

"I understand. Liz told me you didn't want kids."

"I didn't and I never will after this fiasco. People just use the poor children as pawns in their own games. I'll never trust another woman as long as I live."

***

Moments before the phone rang, Liz and Danny stood in the hospital corridor looking through the window of the nursery.

"Look." Liz pointed. "That one's last name is Lovett. They should name him Gotta."

"Gotta Lovett?" Danny laughed. "Poor kid."

It was a little game they played sometimes since the babies' last names were the only ones on their cribs.

"Does Big Daddy look pale to you?" She asked.

"A little. Ever since his heart problems started, his color has looked off to me. I hope he gets healthy and stays that way. I'd like to keep him around a while."

"You and me both, brother."

"He's gonna call, you know."

"Who?" Liz asked

"Ian, who else? Now that he's divorced and it turns out she lied about being pregnant to get him to marry her, he's free to call you."

Her heart slammed against her ribs with the force of fighter's jab. "He better not call me."

"Come on, Liz. He was duped by her and that agent. Give the guy a break."

"The *guy* broke my heart into a million pieces, in front of the world, over something trivial."

"Hey, millions of dollars isn't trivial." He raised a brow.

The truth was she'd give it all away if should could have Ian back. But no, he'd hurt her and humiliated her. She wasn't willing to go there again. He could keep the paparazzi and she'd take her quiet little life at the beach.

Danny's phone rang. "Speak of the devil."

Danny put Ian on speaker phone when he answered, so Liz heard every word.

"Told you so." She mouthed to her brother.

"Ian, Liz is here with me. Would you like to speak to her?"

Liz frantically shook her head. She should've known her brother would pull a stunt like this.

"I'd love to hear her voice. Even if she lets me have it, quite rightly."

She took the phone from her brother, but left it on speaker.

"Hey, Ian. I was sorry to hear about your divorce. Better luck next time." The false sincerity in her voice made her cringe.

"I'm not sorry about it. I'm only sorry the marriage happened in the first place. Bloody lying women."

"Hey, I resemble that remark."

"I didn't mean you. How are you, by the way, you sound different? Are you sick or something?"

"Or something. Have you started filming your new movie?"

"Yes, it's great fun. Everything I always imagined."

"I'm very happy for you. Listen, don't do me any favors and invite me to the premiere. Those days are over."

He chuckled. "Understood."

"Well, Ian, I have to go, but good luck. I know you'll do great."

"Thank you, Liz. You always did believe in me. I should have believed in you more."

"Live and learn. Goodbye, Ian." She held the phone out to her brother, closed her eyes and took a deep breath. The scab on her heart had been ripped off and she was left exposed and bleeding. Part of her wished it would kill her and then he'd be sorry. But, she had too much to live for. The pain subsided. There was no room for it in her life anymore.

CHAPTER THIRTY-THREE

More than a year passed before Ian caught Danny at home. He was beginning to think he'd moved, but late one night he saw the lights on. Not a day went by that he didn't think of Liz, but she'd made it clear when they last spoke that she wanted nothing to do with him. *Those days are over*. Her words resounded in his head.

Hoping for a glimpse of his old friend, he crossed both their gardens. When he got close, he heard Danny's voice.

"Don't shoot, mate." Ian stepped onto the deck. "I saw your light on and thought I'd pop over to say hello."

"Hey, Ian, how's it going?" Danny stood and shook his hand. "You remember my sister, Lizabelle?"

Ian's heart stopped and then skipped a beat or two before resuming a shaky rhythm. Heat spread through his chest and his hands trembled at the sight of her in the dim light.

"Liz, I'm sorry I didn't see you there in the shadows." Without thinking, he bent to hug her. "You are skin and bones. What have you done?"

"That's what happens when—" Danny began.

"You work with a trainer," Liz finished, cutting her brother off.

"You want a beer?" Danny asked.

"Sure, mate, just one. I have an early day tomorrow. Working on a new film and the show."

With Danny gone momentarily, Ian thought of a thousand things he wanted to say to Liz, but not one of them left his lips. He sat across from her, staring into the shadows of her face. She scratched her neck.

"Here you go." Danny handed him a bottle.

"Where've you been, mate?"

"We're just back from Hawaii." Danny sat on the arm of Liz's chair. "Believe it or not, Jason remarried. It took the right woman and a little convincing, but he bit the bullet."

"I do find that difficult to believe. I thought he'd be pining away for Liz until he was old and gray." *Like I will be.* "How are things in Atlanta, Liz? How's the job?"

"I have a new job now." She looked to the back door of the house.

Ian turned, but didn't see anything. "Oh?"

"Yeah, I moved from Atlanta. Congratulations on your movie's success. I hear you have more in the works."

"Yes, thank you. The success of the first film brought a lot of offers. That and having an agent I can trust. I cannot believe you left Atlanta. Is your family still at Southland?" He had learned the art of redirecting conversations from her.

"Yes, they are. We visit as often as we can."

"We?"

"Um..." She cleared her throat. "I have a new man in my life."

"Good for you." He dug his nails into his palm. He was supposed to be the man in her life.

"Ian," an irritatingly high pitched voice called. "Where are you?"

Oh God, he'd forgotten about her. He stood. "I'll be right there."

"She sounds...young." Danny raised an eyebrow.

"The young ones don't want to bear your children just yet." He wanted to tell Liz she was the only woman he'd consider having children with, but it was impossible for her and she had a new man in her life. She wouldn't want to hear it.

Instead, he said, "Thanks for the beer. It was good to see you both."

***

A little more than two years had passed since he'd seen Liz, but Ian was thinking about her when his phone rang. He always thought of her, always missed her.

"Bryan, hello, how are things on the east coast?"

"It's hot, but it's awesome man. I love it over here. Listen, I know you're planning to take some time off for the first time in forever. I was wondering if you might like to come for a visit?"

"Where are you again? Florida?"

"Almost. The nearest airport is in Florida unless you own your own plane. I'm still filming, but I'd like the company. Plus, I think you might like what you find when you get here."

Ian immediately thought of Liz and the flights they'd taken on her family's private planes. "If it's women you're trying to push on me, there are plenty here. I do all right on my own."

"Not women, Ian. A woman."

"What woman?"

"Does the name Liz Baker ring any bells?"

Ian's heart began to beat faster and he sat down hard onto the nearest chair. "What about Liz?"

"She lives here. I saw her playing guitar with a band on the beach."

"Did you speak to her?"

"Duh. I bought her a drink and we talked for a while. Mostly about me when I think back. She has a way of getting you to talk about yourself."

"I know. What did she say? Is she seeing anyone?" He was up pacing the floor.

Bryan laughed. "You sound even more anxious than I thought. I knew you were still in love with her. It's a good thing we're friends or I'd hit on her myself."

"You'll do no such thing. Tell me, please, Bryan, how is she?" Ian could hear the desperation in his own voice.

"Well, she's not dating anybody, but she didn't tell me that. I asked around. She said her day job is twenty-four hours a day, seven days a week so she started playing with the band to make herself take a break."

"That's odd. She never worked like that before. She must be onto a new computer project."

"It's the same thing you've been doing for the last, what, three years. You bury yourself in your work so you won't have to miss the one that got away."

"You're more clever than I give you credit for. I'll see you in two weeks."

CHAPTER THIRTY-FOUR

Liz was finally settled in her new house. She had her dream job and a new life; one where the media had forgotten about her and she could live peacefully with a beautiful view of the Atlantic Ocean. She was a ginger again, but kept blonde highlights, just for fun.

Her big brother was her part-time neighbor. He split his time between the coasts, but having his own wings made it easier to bear the burden. It was only a few hours drive to Southland, less if they flew, so her family came down when they could and she made the trip up there for most holidays and Georgia football games.

She enjoyed playing with a local band on Friday nights and sometimes performed on a dinner boat cruise. She'd missed her music since she'd given up her gig with Jason and found him a replacement. It turned out the waitress, Roxanne, from the bar in Atlanta was also a singer and she played guitar a little. They were great together which was why Jason married her. He adopted her son and they had a baby together.

Liz had only experienced a minor setback in her

mission to get over Ian when she'd seen him at Danny's house in L.A. She wasn't sure if time healed wounds, but it certainly lessened them. One thing she did know was that love healed. She smiled as she watched the love of her life build a sand castle with her niece and nephew.

Liz cooed at the baby she held in her arms and sang a lullaby. In her mind, Ian was next to her, like he'd been when she sang her nieces and nephews to sleep a few summers before. She always looked over her shoulder for him, feeling him near, but he was never there.

Looking out at the ocean, she wiped a tear from her eye. In her life, she'd known love. She swallowed hard before she turned to her companions.

She passed Jason's baby back to him. "She's precious. She has your eyes."

"Yes, but thankfully the rest of her features are her mama's." Jason beamed at his wife. "She *is* perfect, isn't she?"

Liz grabbed her guitar. She was truly happy for him. "Spoken like a proud papa. I'm thrilled for you, Jason. You have a sweet little family and a strong wife to put up with your mess."

"He's not so bad." Roxanne winked at her husband.

Liz knew it was true and she picked an old Eagles tune called *Wasted Time*. Ian invaded her mind, like he always did. Every day was a reminder of what she'd lost with him. Since she'd found out Bryan Watson was in town filming a movie, Ian was more on her mind than ever. She kept thinking she saw him every time she turned around.

***

Ian arrived on the east coast on Saturday and Bryan spent the morning showing him around the small coastal town of Quiet Cove where his movie was being filmed. Ian learned Breck Stanton had a home there. He'd been a big competitor for roles when Ian first began getting movie leads, and he'd never been friendly toward Ian.

He tried not to be impatient, but he really wanted to do what he'd come here for. He patted his pocket for the millionth time.

"I've been doing some recon," Bryan said as he pulled the convertible into a parking space at the hotel. "I found out that Liz usually spends her afternoons on the beach with some friends and their kids."

"What are we waiting for?"

"Afternoon." Bryan crossed his eyes.

Bryan was right about the weather being hot. After lunch, they both took their shoes off and walked down the beach. Ian let the water wash over his feet and it was like a warm bath. It took him back to the summer at Southland when he and Liz spent their nights swimming in the warm water of the lake. The water may have been warm, but he didn't imagine the fire that burned between them. He closed his eyes and asked God for a miracle. Another chance with Liz.

"I think that's her." Bryan pointed.

Ian looked up to see a small group of people sitting on beach chairs. One of them held a guitar. *Liz.* His chest tightened.

As they approached, Bryan cupped his hands around his mouth. "Hey, Lizzie, I brought you a surprise."

Liz's face paled when her eyes met Ian's. She stood

and in the light of day, he could see how much she'd changed. Her hair was shorter and lighter and her body was leaner, but her beauty still stole his breath.

"Oh my God, it's Bryan Watson and Ian Clarke," a woman said. "Am I dead? I think I might be in heaven." The woman stood with her phone. "I've got to get a picture. Oh God, Liz, I can't believe you know them."

"Here, let me take it." Liz set her guitar on her seat and held out her hand.

"You should be in it," the woman said.

"No thanks, I've had my picture taken enough for one lifetime."

Ian tried not to wince at the implication of her words as he and Bryan posed on either side of the woman. It didn't escape Ian's notice that the other woman didn't seem interested in them, though she was holding a baby in her arms.

"Liz!" Another woman shouted from down the beach as she ran full speed toward the water.

Liz looked in her direction, dropped the phone and ran too. Ian was right behind her. The unknown woman came out of thigh high waves carrying three small children. Liz took one of them from her and Ian took another.

They walked out of the water and the woman pointed to the boy Ian held. "That one's mine, I'll take him."

"Are they both yours?" He asked, passing the child back to his mother.

"Yes, fraternal twins. I'm blessed with double the trouble. Liz, are you and little man okay?"

"Yes, thank you, Jane. You're our hero, as per

usual." Liz rubbed the back of the head of the boy in her arms and kissed his forehead.

Ian heard a voice from the past behind him. "Lizabelle, can I take him?"

Ian turned to see Jason gesturing to the child in Liz's arms. Ian nearly stepped away when he recalled Jason's threat from years before.

"Uncle Jason, I went in the water," the boy said.

"I know, buddy, but you weren't supposed to go without a grown up, were you?"

"No, sir. I'm in trouble, right mama?"

Ian thought he'd heard wrong, until Liz spoke.

"That's right, baby. We have the rules to keep you safe."

Despite the heat of the day, a chill ran over Ian's body. Was this Liz's son? He looked more closely at the small boy. He had long, skinny arms and legs, blond hair, and blue-gray eyes just like...

"Liz," he croaked and squeezed his fingers shut as they began to shake.

"Just breathe, Ian, I can explain, if you'll let me." Liz looked past Ian to Jason. "I think I better keep him with me."

"Do I get a spanking?" the boy asked.

She dropped to her knees on the sand and set the boy on his feet. "Is it enough to know that you scared mama to death?"

The little boy nodded as big tears welled up in his eyes.

"It's okay, sweetheart, don't cry." She wiped away a tear from his cheek. "I'm not mad. I was scared. I just want you to be safe."

The little boy wrapped his arms around Liz's neck

and she stood up holding him.

"I think someone needs a nap. Do you want to join us?" She asked Ian.

"I think I'd better." Ian's voice didn't sound like his own. He took shallow breaths and followed Liz back to the chair where her guitar lay. She reached for a beach bag.

"I'll take it." Ian grabbed it. The sooner he got her alone, the sooner he'd get an explanation.

"We're down this way." She pointed.

Ian walked beside her, never taking his eyes from the little boy whose head rested on Liz's shoulder. The child soon found him interesting as well.

"I'm Ethan." The little boy lifted his head and extended his hand.

Ian's eyes filled with tears and a lump formed in his throat. He choked them back as he took the tiny hand in his. "I'm Ian. It's a pleasure to meet you."

The little boy smiled and Ian's heart turned to mush. It got mushier when Ethan began to sing.

"You're a singer like your mum then?" Ian asked.

"What's a mum?"

Ian explained and rambled on, unsure what he was saying until they approached a large, cottage style house. Liz stopped to shower Ethan off at an outdoor shower. She stripped him out of his swim shorts, left them hanging to dry and wrapped him in a towel.

Ethan's teeth chattered once they entered the air conditioned house. Ian nearly reached out to the boy. The urge to take him in his arms and warm him was so intense.

"Ian, there's Coke in the fridge. The sugar may help with the shock. I'm going to put dry clothes on this one or else he'll streak through the house and freeze his cute little tushy off."

Ian stood frozen with his hand on the refrigerator door while the miniature version of himself disappear up the stairs.

CHAPTER THIRTY-FIVE

Liz's pulse thundered in her ears and she itched all over. She was extremely apprehensive about talking to Ian, especially with Ethan present. She hoped Ian would keep his cool. Ethan ran back into the kitchen to see their visitor and Liz made a quick stop by her desk. She walked into the kitchen and placed a manila envelope on the counter next to where Ian stood.

"I can make a sammich." Ethan told Ian as he stood on his tiptoes with the pantry door open and reached for the peanut butter.

"Allow me." She took the jar. "Why don't you climb up on your stool and I'll get you some milk."

"Milk makes me strong." Ethan took a running leap up onto the seat.

Ian assisted and scooted him closer to the bar. "How old are you?"

Ethan held up three fingers. Liz knew Ian was doing the math. Even though it wasn't perfect, it still timed out pretty close.

"I came early," Ethan said. "What's that word, Mama? It starts with a *p*."

"Premature."

"Permachure," he repeated, making Liz smile.

"You know your letters?" Ian asked.

"Yeah, wanna hear? A, b, c, d...." His new thing was to sing the alphabet song as fast as possible.

Ian smiled when he finished. "Impressive. I bet you can count, too."

"Yes, Sir, I get mixed up sometimes, but I can do it if I keep practicing, right Mama?"

"That's right, baby."

Liz placed half a peanut butter sandwich on a napkin in front of Ethan. She gave the other half to Ian, which he accepted.

She'd been dreading this moment since the first day she peed on a stick. Knowing how Ian felt about having kids, she decided that her son wasn't going to be made to feel unwanted by anyone, so she kept it from him.

She wavered in her decision many times over the years. Especially, when the momentous things happened like his first words or his first steps.

Ethan reached into his shorts' pocket and pulled out two action figures. "You can play with Spiderman. I'll play with Wolverine."

"That's a big deal, Ian. You rank if you get Spiderman. He ties with Wolverine for the top spot."

Ethan drank the last of his milk, wiped his arm across his mouth and yawned.

"You ready for a nap, kiddo?"

He nodded. "Can Mr. Ian carry me?"

"Maybe you should ask him nicely."

He did and Ian stood and picked him up. Liz's heart did a flip in her chest at the sight of her baby in his daddy's arms. She grabbed the envelope and followed them upstairs.

"This is arguably the most fantastic bed I've ever seen," Ian said.

"I like boats." Ethan was proud of his twin size bed shaped like a boat.

"Mama likes it so Captain Ethan doesn't roll out of the bed." Liz pulled the blanket back so Ian could lay him down.

"Mama, tell me a story."

It was a daily ritual they went through at naptime and bedtime. "Which one? The Princess and the Pea?"

"Nooo." Ethan giggled. "That's for girls. Tell the prince from the Motherland story."

Ian looked at her for the first time since they'd gotten to her house. He raised an eyebrow. "This might be a story I'd like to hear."

The weight of his stare was heavy. She deserved it. She'd convinced herself that keeping her son from Ian was the best thing. But now, she questioned everything.

She knelt beside the bed. "Once upon a time, there was an American woman..." She paused so Ethan could sing.

His little fingers played air guitar. "American Woman."

She looked at Ian, but tried not to think too hard about the rest of the lyrics, since the song essentially described her and Ian's breakup. "What can I say? He's a Kravitz fan like his Mama. I shoulda named you Lenny."

He giggled. "No, Eeethan." He made the hurry up gesture with his hand. "She fell in love with a prince from the Motherland."

She cleared her throat. "Right, but they couldn't be together, so the prince gave the woman a very special gift."

Ethan looked at Ian. "Guess."

Ian shrugged. "Ah, was it gold?"

"No, it was a baby. Me." Ethan whispered like he was in a barn. "The evil queen put the prince under a spell."

Liz's face got hot and she couldn't meet Ian's eyes. "Hey, who's telling this story?" She tickled Ethan and he squirmed and giggled.

Ian picked up the thread of the story. "The evil queen tricked the prince. But the prince also fooled himself by thinking anyone or anything other than the American woman could ever satisfy him." He reached out and caressed Liz's face.

She was waiting for his wrath, so the gentle hand disoriented her.

"Am I a prince, Mama?"

"You're my prince and you're my dream come true." Liz took Ethan's hand and kissed his fingertips.

"Do they live happily ever after?" Ethan asked.

"I hope so." Ian took both her hand and Ethan's in his and kissed her.

It was soft and sweet like the first time their lips touched. When he pulled back, her face was wet with tears. She turned so her son couldn't see.

"You love my mama?"

"Very much." Ian cupped her cheek and used his thumb to wipe beneath her eye.

"Are you Spiderman?"

"No, and I'm no prince either, but I'd like to be."

"Me, too." Ethan yawned.

Liz dried her face on her shirt and turned to smile at her baby.

His eyelids fluttered shut. "Sing the song, Mama."

She wasn't sure she could sing with the emotion lodged in her throat. After a moment, Ian sang the lullaby he'd learned from her all those years ago. Ethan's huge smile slowly relaxed as he drifted off to sleep.

***

Ian sat back on his heels next to Liz on the floor by Ethan's bed. He didn't want to leave the little boy's side. Liz handed him a manila envelope and they talked in quiet voices.

"What's this?"

"You told Danny you'd want a paternity test if any woman ever told you they had your child. This is the proof."

He set the envelope aside, unopened. "I don't need proof. I know it in my heart." He took her hand and held it to his chest. "I only wish I'd known sooner although I understand why you didn't trust me."

"How can that be?" Her brow creased between her eyes. "You went off the deep end about a minor lie of omission that I committed and this is...well, it isn't minor."

"You once told me that you extended grace to others because you hoped the day you needed it, they'd extend it back. I had no mercy on you before, but I'm going to be better this time. I have too much to lose." He placed a hand on his son's lower leg.

"Liz, I was selfish. I thought I knew what I wanted and what would make me happy. You did what you thought was right by not telling me about him. As many times as I insisted I didn't want kids, how could you have known that the only woman I'd ever considered having a family with is you?" He took her hand and rubbed circles with his thumb.

She swallowed hard and blinked as tears fell. He wiped them away.

"How did it, I mean, how could it have happened?"

She shrugged. "I didn't even know I was pregnant until twelve weeks in, because I didn't think...I never...I just thought I was heart sick. It turned out to be morning sickness...which sometimes lasted all day."

"That was just after I married Emma and it was all over the news that we were expecting."

She nodded and looked down. "The doctor told me my body must've been ready. All I know is that he's a miracle." She brushed Ethan's hair back with her fingers.

"He's definitely a miracle. He's beautiful. I just have one question for you." He reached into his pocket and held the diamond and sapphire ring out to her. "Liz Baker, I should've proposed years ago. Please agree to be my wife. Please tell me we can be a family." He slid the ring onto her finger.

"Ian, I...I have to think about what's best for Ethan. I would love for you to be in our lives, but I can't...I'm not good at the celebrity thing."

"I'd give it all up to have you both in my life. I did what I set out to do. Now, I can work when and if I want. There's only one more season of *Trauma*. I'll tell them to kill me off early." He held her hand in both of his. "Plus, unless something's changed, you can support our family." He pressed his lips together to contain his laugh.

She snorted. "I've still got a little in the bank." Her smile faded. "Are you sure you're willing to give it up, Ian? I don't want you to resent us." Her gaze flicked to their son.

"My regrets outweigh any resentment I may have felt. I regret not having you and Ethan in my life for the past four years. I've missed you every day. Please say yes."

She smiled. "I need to talk to him first."

"Can we talk to him together?"

Liz leaned over and kissed Ethan on his forehead and stood to go. Ian did the same, but lingered a bit, not wanting to leave his son. His heart was so full, he thought it might burst.

Ian wanted to know everything Ethan had ever said and done. Liz pulled up a photo file on her computer and walked him through from Ethan's premature birth to his recent third Birthday party. His selfishness had caused him to miss so much—the really important things in life. His stomach knotted as he skimmed a finger across a Baker family Christmas picture.

"What will your family think of me?" She asked.

He blinked. "I'm worried about what the Bakers think of me, too. Mine knows how adamant I've been against having children, so they won't blame you. They'll be dying to meet him. First though, I'd like to get to know him better myself. Do you think he'll...like me?"

"When I tell him you're the prince who gave him to me and you finally got out from under the spell of the evil queen, he'll worship you."

Ian pulled Liz into his lap for a passion-filled kiss and it was like they'd never been apart. His Southern belle had penetrated his heart and soul. "God, I've missed you."

He would've tried to find her bedroom in another moment had he not heard the sound of little feet coming down the stairs.

Liz gave Ian's leg a reassuring squeeze and turned to Ethan, holding her arms open. He ran and jumped up into her lap and she wrapped him in a bear hug.

"Did you get your nap out, sweetpea?"

"Yes, ma'am. I had a good dream." He threw his head back and smiled at her with his hands clasped behind her neck. "I love you, Mama."

"I'm the luckiest woman in the world. I love you too, my little smooch monster." She placed kisses on his face, neck, arms, and legs while making smooch noises. He giggled and wriggled in her arms and made smooch noises back at her.

Ian wanted in on the action, but didn't know how to insert himself into their duo.

"I think he needs some smooches from the smooch monster." Liz tipped her head toward Ian.

"Let's get him." Ethan squealed and climbed from Liz to Ian's lap.

Ian took instruction from Liz as he practiced the smooch noise and placed little kisses on his son. After a moment, he squeezed his eyes shut. His throat was tight, making swallowing difficult.

Ethan stopped wiggling in his arms and placed his small hands on each side of Ian's face. "Are those happy tears or sad tears?"

Ian opened his eyes to see his son looking into his face and searching his expression for an answer. He was smart, probably a genius like his mum, and also perceptive.

"Very happy tears." His voice threatened to break.

Ethan used his little thumbs and rubbed at the corners of Ian's eyes.

"Baby, I have something to tell you. You know our story about the Motherland? Well..." Liz explained.

"If you're the prince, then are you my daddy?" Ethan's eyes were big.

Ian nodded and swallowed. "I am."

"Yay!" Ethan wrapped his arms tightly around Ian's neck.

Ian thought he might lose his breath, but he didn't care. Other than having Liz's arms around him, nothing had ever been sweeter.

"Baby, don't choke your daddy." Liz pulled at his arm.

"Are you gonna come live with us? You can stay in my room." Ethan put his feet in Ian's lap and bounced.

"There's nothing I want more in this world than to be with you...and to marry your mum." Ian took Liz's left hand and lifted it to show Ethan the ring. "I asked, but she hasn't given me her answer."

"We should say yes, Mama."

EPILOGUE

The ceremony was very small and very private. Well, as small as it could be considering the bride and groom came from such large families. They were married at Southland on the end of the dock near sunset. Ethan and Big Daddy both gave Liz away. No paparazzi showed up.

All of the Clarkes came from England and Jacqueline and Simon spent a month at Southland with their newfound grandson whom they loved instantly. To Liz's surprise and relief, they never once chided her for keeping him from Ian or them.

The wedding picture they later framed and hung in their Los Angeles, Quiet Cove, and London residences was of Ian holding Ethan in one arm with the other wrapped around his wife. The sky was salmon pink fading to gray at the tree line. Both boys were looking lovingly down at their leading lady.

Ian's vow included this admission: "Liz, you are the one who made my fairy tale come true. You've fulfilled dreams I never had until I met you. This fairy tale doesn't end."

After the ceremony, they had cake and ice cream at

the main house. Ethan spent the night there with his grandparents and cousins while the newlyweds stayed in the cottage closest to the lake. Late that night, Ian and Liz shared a bottle of wine, a swim, and a dance in the moonlight.

ABOUT THE AUTHOR

Meda White is an award-winning author who writes sweet, funny, southern romance. Born with Georgia clay running through her veins, she continues to enjoy the heat and humidity of the South with her Hubba-luv and furbabies—Lily, a very sweet yet spoiled Collie, and Lulu, the cat with one fang. When not writing, you might find her making music, shooting zombie targets, teaching fitness, or explaining the meaning of her unusual first name.

DEDICATION

To Hubba-luv—
Thank you for loving me more.
We both win.

ACKNOWLEDGMENTS

Thank you to the members of Southern Magic for
the advice, encouragement, and support.
And a big thanks to all of my English teachers.
Your many lessons are of great value.

OTHER BOOKS BY MEDA WHITE

The Southland Romance Series

Play With My Heart: A Southland Romance 1

Dance With My Heart: A Southland Romance 2

Ride With My Heart: A Southland Romance 3

Fool With My Heart: A Southland Romance 4

Home With My Heart: A Southland Romance
(The Prequel)

The Southern College Novellas

Spring Fling

Fall Rush

Winter Formal

Standalone

Christmas Give

A NOTE TO READERS

Dear Reader,

Thank you for reading *Play With My Heart*. I hope you enjoyed Liz and Ian's love story. If you're interested in the other Southland Romances, you'll get to see more of Liz and Ethan.

If you have a moment to leave an honest review, I'd really appreciate it. Not only do reviews let authors know how they're doing, they help readers find new books. I love to hear from readers. Please look for me on my Website and at my Facebook Group *Meda's Dirt Road Darlings*.

Thank you, and best wishes for a lifetime of love and laughter. Oh, and don't forget to play every now and then.

Meda